I Tagged Her in my Heart

A TEDx speaker and marketing consultant settled in Mumbai, **Anuj Tiwari** was brought up on the bustling streets of Bareilly, where chaos is the order of the day. There, he learnt to circumvent the streets first, and then his convoluted life. Instead of getting a 'modern education', Tiwari studied in a Sanskrit-medium school where there were no English books. Seeing his neighbourhood kids reading from colourful storybooks, he started building dreams of being able to read in English; however, he kept those dreams to himself in the fear of being mocked at.

Tiwari, who has seen his family go through a tough time and being humiliated in his childhood, was thus encouraged to push the limits.

Despite going through six months of depression and trying to give up on his life in college, Tiwari is now the bestselling author of three books. He sold his books on the streets of Mumbai, and has been listed as one of the top ten most influential authors in India in 2016.

I Tagged Her in My Heart is Anuj Tiwari's most personal creation, inspired by his own life.

Other bestsellers by Anuj Tiwari

Journey of Two Hearts!

It Had to Be You

It's Not Right...but It's Okay

I Tagged Her in my Heart

ANUJ TIWARI

RUPA

Published by
Rupa Publications India Pvt. Ltd 2018
7/16, Ansari Road, Daryaganj
New Delhi 110002

Sales centres:

Allahabad Bengaluru Chennai
Hyderabad Jaipur Kathmandu
Kolkata Mumbai

This is a work of fiction. Names, characters, places and incidents are either the product of the author's imagination or are used fictitiously and any resemblance to any actual person, living or dead, events or locales is entirely coincidental.

ISBN: 978-81-291-4956-5

Third impression 2018

10 9 8 7 6 5 4 3

Printed at Thomson Press India Ltd., Faridabad

To

Dimpy Aunty and my mom without whom
I would probably
have completed this book a year ago

Wait! You know how it is. You pick up a book, flip to the dedication, and find out, once again, that the author has dedicated this book to someone else and not you.

Not this time.

We may, or may not, have met each other. However, I feel that we share a good bond. Just because of you, I exist. I am thankful to have you in my life. Moreover, I believe that we will meet some day for sure. Till then, I am gifting this story to you. This one is for you.

Just not to spoil the story, I would rather say, everything is going to be okay in the end.

Prologue

Every relationship has its cycle. It starts with a meeting. You meet someone, and then you want to meet that person more. Later, one day, you realize that you are in love with that person.

You count that person in everything and start making plans for the future. You anticipate their calls, want to hear their voice and want to feel their touch. You start liking their idiosyncrasies and quirks.

Falling in love with someone is the best thing that happens to you and one of the best feelings in the world. You just go with the flow of emotions. You just follow wherever it takes you. That is why we say, 'we *fall* in love.'

In the journey of love, you reach a point where you think that the person is the right one for you.

When you are in love, you feel you are being swept off your feet. Imagine the expression. You are just there—standing, doing nothing and then some day, SOMETHING happens to you.

Falling in love with someone is an impulsive and spontaneous feeling. However, what is more important is what happens after that. You never think about it. But, after a few months, or years, of being together, the ecstasy and excitement of love fade. That is quite natural and happens in EVERY relationship.

Everything happens very slowly, but this time, you are on the other side. Gradually, those phone calls, which you used to wait for eagerly, become a bother or duty to answer. Touch, which used to make you shiver, now becomes irritable. It does not excite you as it did earlier.

Moreover, the idiosyncrasies and quirks, which you always appreciated and accepted in all forms, start grating and bothering you so much that it feels like a knife slicing through your head.

When you start noticing the changes in your relationship—how it was initially and how it is now—you find a big and stagy difference. You start seeing the relationship as a 'burden' that you keep dragging.

Your partner and you start asking yourselves, 'Am I the right person to be loved?' On the other hand, most importantly, a question flicks into your mind, 'Am I with the right person?'

We are all humans, and share a similar nature. You may wish or desire to feel the same love you had with someone else. That is the time when most breakups happen. Family consent and caste difference just become excuses to break away from that relationship.

Most of the time, people say that they are not happy—they blame their partners and look for happiness in others—and end up having extramarital affairs. Infidelity is very common in relationships these days.

A few people may end up finding someone better outside their relationship but the truth and the reality of this dilemma lie within the relationship, NOT outside.

There is no rule that you cannot fall in love with someone else, that is also natural. You feel the same or even better than your previous relationship. But this is temporary. Years later, you will find yourself in a similar situation and start feeling miserable once again. You will realize it was all an illusion, but by then it would be too late, and you may have already ruined too many things.

So instead of finding the answer to, 'Am I with the right person?', you should try to understand that a successful and lifelong relationship is not about finding the right person, but about learning to love the person you have already found. That is not easy, by the way.

Successful relationships are not really spontaneous and impulsive experiences. You have to put effort, work on it each day. They are just like the giant trees with deep roots, as much time and work go into growing them. They aren't like the small plants, weak and timid.

A sustaining love takes time, effort and energy. You should not see it as a liability or an asset, but you should know what you have to do to make it work and where you have to take this relationship. MAKE NO MISTAKES ABOUT IT.

Loving someone is not tough, but the real challenge is to be with that person forever, with happiness and faith. That is important.

Love is neither an illusion nor a mystery. It is just like the few basics of your favourite subject. If you know how to apply them, you start getting the results—the expected positive results that you wish for.

Therefore, love is a *decision*, not just a *feeling*.

Maybe God determines who walks into our life. However, it is up to us to decide who we let walk away, who we let stay and who we refuse to let go!

One

EVERYONE GOES THROUGH a tough time in life, but it becomes even tougher for Arjun when he tries to make his mother understand that he has grown up and can take decisions in his life.

According to her, he will always be a kid. Whatever he does, is wrong.

Arjun is one of those victims of Indian mothers. If he is not even allowed to take his own decisions, how would she ever know whether he is capable to make the right decisions or not? Well, nothing works in front of her.

Arjun was born in a Brahmin family, headed by a mother who is suspicious, overprotective and overcaring for him.

He has grown up in a family where he had to chant the bhojan mantra before having food. He is from a school where teachers were like celebrities; they rarely made an appearance in class! Therefore, this is not new to him. His life has just turned weirder over a period.

There were many other things which were more dramatic, except that he preferred to learn things from his elders rather than from books. That has made him different in the family. However, when he told his mother that he wanted to do something different in life, his mom slapped him, and he was back to his studies.

Moreover, when he grew up, he realized that in Indian families, if your neighbour's child is an engineer or a doctor, you have to be one as well. Unfortunately, Arjun had both. So, looking at the return on investment (ROI), his mom decided that he should study to become an engineer, though he was interested in biology. His friends tease him now that this interest in biology is probably the inspiration behind the way he describes romantic scenes.

Arjun is an author and lives in Mumbai. Though he is a grown-up now, his mother still has some obligations. She says that she has all the right to do so. After all, she is an Indian mother, and for them, insecurity is a constant companion. She is constantly worrying about him and diligently tracks his online as well as offline activities. She thinks he is too emotional and can be trapped easily. Well, the grass is always greener on the other side. She hasn't seen the other side of him. She should see him when he is with his friends—entertaining, crazy and funny.

Overall, Arjun has lived his life exactly like every other Indian son or daughter. Primarily because he always finds his mother around, questioning about what is right and wrong. From selecting crayons in school to choosing an organization to work, his mother has always had a vital role to play in his life. Fortunately for him, all her decisions have worked out well. That is why every day his phone beeps at 10 p.m. with her call, no matter where he is, and in whichever corner of the world.

As always, Arjun has just had an argument with his mom over the phone—that he doesn't want to get married now. At twenty-six, marriage is the last thing on his mind! 'But the permanent entry of a girl in your life will make things easier for you,' she had argued. She is probably right, but he still needs time.

Sitting near the sliding window of his room, he is in deep thought.

Arjun's phone flashes a call from Dimpy Aunty. He swipes left on the screen and disconnects the call.

♥

Dimpy Aunty is like a shadow. When God created happiness, he also created a few Indian aunties to balance that out. Arjun thinks Dimpy Aunty is one of them.

Everyone has that one Aunty who is just born to poke her nose into everything.

Arjun is suffering from aunty-phobia, as it were. Sometimes it's really funny when they both argue with each other, but they cannot live apart.

Dimpy Aunty is his best friend Anushka's mother. After his last argument with Anushka, he has changed the contact name for Dimpy Aunty on his phone. He now realizes that the new contact name sounds like one of those naughty American video clips—My Best Friend's Mother.

Since college, Anushka has always helped him out in his personal as well as professional life.

She was a year senior to him; and after receiving her engineering degree, she joined Vccenture Services in Bengaluru as a Business Analyst. A year later, Arjun joined the same company at its Mumbai office.

Frustrated with her nine-to-six job, Anushka had quit to pursue an MBA from IIFT in Delhi.

Now, she works as a marketing manager at a firm in Mumbai, living with her family. Over time, their friendship has grown stronger, and now Arjun has both Dimpy Aunty and Anushka to count on.

Dimpy Aunty is sometimes the coolest person to be with, but most of the time, a critic of Arjun. You cannot argue with her. There are only two outcomes of any argument with Dimpy Aunty—either accept the defeat or go to hell. Arjun has equal scores in both.

When, a few years ago, Arjun went through a tragic breakup and was suffering from depression, it was Anushka and Dimpy Aunty who helped him through that bitter six-month phase.

Anushka and Arjun are like soul siblings. They know almost everything about each other, sometimes more than what a friend should. She goes shopping with him. He shares all his problems with her. He drops her home after nights out in clubs. Sometimes she wakes him up early in the morning and then they continue to talk till late in the evening. They have shared the same glass of drink, even the same bed, but they are just friends. The best of friends.

Neither his mother nor Dimpy Aunty knows about it. However, they know everything else about them.

♥

Arjun pulls his luggage to the corner of the room and sets four alarms for 5.10, 5.13, 5.15 and 5.17. That is necessary if he plans to wake up at 5.30 a.m. Tomorrow, 10 July, is a big day. Arjun has to leave for his first TEDx talk that he has been invited for.

His phone rings again. There is a well-known fact, which, somehow, is not applicable to these two people in this world—a mother and a girlfriend. If someone disconnects your call, it means he will call back when he can. But, in his life, those two people—his mother and Dimpy Aunty—would continue to call him, until he takes the call.

Disinterested, he takes her call.

'Why were you not picking my call? I got worried. How are you?' Dimpy Aunty shoots a string of questions. First, he didn't want to pick her call and second, it does not matter to him if she is worried because she is always worried for no reason, and third, he is just nervous. Not because of the speech he has to deliver tomorrow but because he has acrophobia and it has been raining too much in Mumbai. He is scared of the turbulence in flight.

'I am fine,' he says dryly.

'Good. For how many days are you staying in Mohali?' she asks in excitement, probably thinking he will bring back a present for her.

'Two days,' says Arjun. No change in his tone.

'But you have a one-day event, right? Is there anyone special with whom you have planned something?' She is getting her pace and trying to make him confess.

'There is no one, Aunty. How's Mom?' Arjun tries to change the topic.

Dimpy Aunty and his mother talk regularly on the phone these days. Though he has no idea what they really talk about.

'She is all good. We both are enjoying the shopping sales these days.'

'Yes, Dad told me that he is only getting notifications of transactions these days,' Arjun replies.

'Sarcasm, hmm...' she laughs. 'So did they sponsor the trip?'

'No, the publisher has done that.'

'Can't I write? Isn't it cool that you write a few books and the publisher sponsors your trips, and you get a chance to visit places and meet people?'

'Quite true. Yes, you can,' Arjun says. He could never be rude to her.

'Arjun it's okay. Don't be nervous. I am just trying to divert your mind. You have that much fear of turbulence?' she giggles.

'Don't laugh Aunty,' Arjun walks to the window to check

whether it is still raining heavily or not. It is.

'I like turbulence,' she chuckles some more.

'Don't do that. It's raining so much for the last three days,' Arjun seems to be only interested in discussing rains and wants her to make him believe that it will not rain the following day.

'Okay, leave it. So, are you prepared with the speech? What are you going to speak about?' She is curious.

'Nothing to prepare as such. I will share from whatever I have gone through over the years. Anyway, the creepy fact is much better than the artificial one,' Arjun says and takes a long look outside the window.

'That's my boy,' Aunty says in a cheerful tone, an attempt to boost his spirit.

Arjun is a simple guy who believes that goodness is still alive in humans, that true love still exists if you find the right person and that you reap what you sow. He, however, has not found the right one yet. Sometimes, when he feels his principles are too idealistic, he assures himself that there is always a right time for the right thing. Maybe he has a plausible explanation for his beliefs. However, his mother is worried because of these very beliefs. Sometimes she asks him why he becomes so emotional with girls. He just blinks at her. That's a blink of worry for her.

'Well, I have something to tell you, your mom is coming to Mumbai to surprise you on Monday. So clean the house. Tell your roommates to throw away the bottles, if any. And all the best for tomorrow.'

'Thanks!' says Arjun, feeling much better now.

Arjun was expecting this surprise visit from his mom after her trip to Goa with his Nanu and elder sister, who is getting married later this year. His sister Neerja thinks that this is the right time to spend all her savings before she discloses it to her fiancé.

Neither is his mother a globetrotter nor does she want Arjun to travel without any reason, apart from his book signing sessions and other events. It was his Nanu's wish to go to Goa. This is the least a daughter can do for her father at the age of sixty before he takes his final ride to the other world forever.

His Nanu has just turned sixty, but the older he gets, the more liberal he becomes. This is what Arjun has come to understand. This singular and surprising aspect of his ageing has brought them closer in the last few years. Arjun feels lucky to have a grandparent who gets better with age, just like fine wine, and with whom he can discuss his life openly without any reservations. He switches off the lights and goes off to sleep.

♥

The next day Arjun leaves for the city of curd and butter—Chandigarh. As he joins the queue at the check-in desk, he sees groups of people talking about the inclement weather in Mumbai. They seem excited, their faces brim with happiness. 'Probably everyone does not wish to live,' he ponders.

He tries to develop a virtual relationship with the passengers who are standing in the same queue. In crisis, our own people help us. He is trying hard. He knows he will miss Anushka. She had promised to come with him. They had made plans to roam about in the beautiful city, but her change of mind had dampened his mood.

'She always does this at the last moment,' he murmurs as he boards the flight.

Arjun feels the thrum of the engines during take-off and the vibration of the plane during the flight on his skin.

While he pushes himself to the chair with a fastened

seatbelt, the flight takes off with jet speed. He closes his eyes and prays for his safety.

The flight becomes stable in a few moments. The earth has turned into a Google map screen now when he peeps out of the window.

'What happened?' a young girl sitting next to him taps on his hand softly, raising her eyebrows in naughtiness and blinking.

'Nothing,' he simply replies. Nothing really comes out when you are in fear.

'Are you afraid of travelling in flight or turbulence?' she grins at him, and her babbling voice does not really ease his fear.

'No, no, I am good,' seizing himself in the seat, he says confidently. All she can find is the fear in his eyes.

His fear gets nastier when he plays the videos that Dimpy Aunty has sent him coincidently on WhatsApp—Top 10 Plane Crashes—when the flight is about to take off.

He goes through the message from Anushka wishing him good luck and with a fake yawn, pretending to be sleepy, shuts his eyes.

The end of every turbulence seems to give him a new life. He closes his eyes and waits for the flight to land.

♥

There is an air of excitement as Arjun lands in Chandigarh. The afternoon is buzzing with possibilities. As always, he imagines the new faces he will meet, the new experiences and, probably, a new story.

Dragging his trolley bag through the lobby to his hotel room, he feels that he should perhaps listen to Dimpy Aunty and get into a relationship. She says this is the best time to be in a relationship. Travelling is a hobby common to most girls, and he can take them out on sponsored trips. He takes his phone out and reads the message flashing on the screen. That's Dimpy Aunty—

All the best. Love you as always.

He smiles thinking that she will never change. He replies.

Thank you! You are the last person I would ever hate.

Dimpy Aunty typing...

Take care.

Thanks! See you.

Dimpy Aunty has two daughters and no son. Maybe she sees a son in Arjun. His relationship with Dimpy Aunty can't be defined; he feels safe and at home when she is around. Arjun's mother says that he is emotional not just with girls but with every one of the female breed.

Arjun is lucky to have two mothers in his life. However, both are suspicious and sarcastic about his deeds and actions.

Two

AFTER A WONDERFUL time at the event, Arjun spends some time with the few friends he has made just a few hours ago. While at lunch, he gets a call from Ved that he disconnects knowing dining ethics.

'Knowing the etiquette makes you a gentleman'—Anushka has told him several times.

He behaves like a gentleman now. He receives a message from Ved asking him to call him as soon as possible as it's urgent.

Arjun excuses himself from the lunch table to make the call because Ved is someone who only calls in an emergency.

Arjun and Ved have been flatmates for more than a year in Mumbai.

Arjun, Anushka and Ved used to study in the same college. They both had come to Mumbai as engineers, but Ved could not keep up with his jobs. He didn't want to keep up with them either. They were good friends in college, but after college, everyone got busy with their lives. They were not in touch for several months. Just two months before Ved started looking for a place to live, Arjun landed up in Mumbai. Anushka happened to know that they both were looking for a place and suggested that they get a place together.

Therefore, they rekindled their friendship, but could never rekindle the bond they shared in college. Things change over time.

Ved was chasing his dream of playing football for India.

As there is very less encouragement for football in India,

he ended up being a freelance football coach for multiple small teams including a few Mumbai clubs.

Ved travels a lot and that is why Arjun is happy sharing his place with him. He has more space to himself than what he had expected.

'Arjun! How are you?'

'I am good. You called me to ask this?' Arjun questions in sarcasm. He has left his dessert on the table for this!

'Trying to crack a witty joke. Well, I have something to tell you,' his voice goes down like a sinusoidal wave.

'Mom is coming tomorrow morning? I know that,' he replies as if he has some divine power, thanks to Dimpy Aunty.

'You didn't tell me that,' Ved says before adding, 'Adrika is coming today.'

'What? Mumbai? When?' Arjun asks, ignoring everyone around. Stunned and thrilled. Few people turn to look at him.

'Yeah, she has messaged me on Facebook and told me she will reach Mumbai this evening. You should be here.'

'For how many days?' he asks in anticipation. His friends at the lunch table call out to him. He smiles and tells them he will join them in a minute.

'No idea. When are you coming?' asks Ved.

'Very soon. Bye, I will see you there. Don't tell her that I am coming.'

Keeping dining ethics aside, he cancels his scheduled flight ticket to Mumbai and books another one for early morning. He realizes how easy it is to write off a sponsored ticket. He smiles and finishes one of the happiest lunches thinking about Adrika. They are going to meet after years.

♥

Arjun reaches in the morning. His mother has arrived an hour earlier and is already busy in the kitchen.

Times have changed, and only fortunate people have the blessing to see their mother when they get home after office, college or any trip. Though it's a matter of only a few days, Arjun is happy with this joyful and affectionate change. Things become easier for him when he has his mother around.

'Ved, who has kept wine bottles in the kitchen?' asks Arjun's mother.

Arjun and Ved exchange looks sitting in the hall while his mom prepares salad in the kitchen. She loves to spend time in the kitchen for Arjun and her family. That is what she has done for all the years—taken care of everyone. That is where she has found her happiness in though Arjun has questioned her many times to hear the other side of her life. He has got nothing except a smiling face or, at the max, a few sarcastic words.

'Mummy, sometimes, I think of writing something about you one day, why don't you tell me your story? I have asked you so many times,' following her footsteps to the kitchen, Arjun tries to divert the question she has asked.

She replies positively, 'Maybe when you become more famous one day.' She always gives him hopes and possibilities and strengthens him. She just gets worried about him at times. We only worry about the people we love.

'But still…why don't you tell me everything…' Arjun repeats.

'I was married at the age of sixteen, that will be the opening line for your book,' and she repeats, 'Ved, who has kept wine bottles in the kitchen?'

Arjun curses Ved because that was his responsibility.

♥

Arjun knows how cleaning the house before his mother's arrival was almost like running a marathon. It was a planned trip, but, as usual, his mother took a detour to give him a surprise. She wanted to see how Arjun and Ved live. She would surely come to know if the house matched up to the descriptions relayed over the phone.

'You said these bottles look beautiful. So I have kept them,' Ved responds and questions peeping into the kitchen, 'What to do now?'

'No, just keep quiet, I'll manage.'

Nanu sitting in the corner near the window looks at Arjun and Ved. 'I hope everything is going well here,' he says.

'Yes, everything is fine,' Ved reverts instantly.

'Now, I have also lived with friends in Kolkata for a long time. So just saying,' Nanu says with fewer words.

Arjun settles things, putting all the blame on Ved and late-night visits by his friends, although he has also been a part of those, having a few sips with them.

Ved goes to the kitchen and returns after a minute.

'I have cleared everything,' he murmurs.

'So quickly!' Arjun says sarcastically, giving him a weird look. His mom appears following Ved to the hall holding a bottle in her hand. She looks serious, 'Who has left this in the fridge?' Arjun looks at Ved.

'You can't grow plants in these bottles in the fridge, can you?' she holds out the bottle filled with water and a money plant. It is actually a water bottle with weed in it. Arjun does not know what Ved wants to do with it.

'Oh sorry, I was cleaning the kitchen so left the bottle inside,' Arjun replies highlighting that he has cleaned the kitchen, though it does not look like it.

'And what about this? Who is responsible for this?' she shows him the bottle. There is some wine left in it.

'Oh, another bottle for money plant. I have no interest in growing herbs and plants. Ved must know,' Arjun redirects her to Ved. He can't save him anymore for his continuous mistakes.

'No, Aunty I think few of our friends left it there. Give it to me, I'll throw it out,' Ved dumps the bottle into the bin.

'Your friends are forgetting things at your place too frequently,' she glares at Arjun.

'If I would have done that, you would be the first person I would tell,' Arjun says. It means a lot to her. He must be the luckiest boy in his family without any pressure from his parents. All they want in return is trust. She has no fear of Arjun lying to her because she is sure to catch him in no time. From time to time, she keeps asking the household help, either on phone or during her visits about how Arjun and Ved live. She knows everything—told and untold.

♥

'Arjun, you have turned twenty-seven,' she says approaching him, carrying a bowl in her hands. She serves food to all.

'Mom, twenty-six, not twenty-seven, that is only written in my school certificates, not the birth certificate. Moreover, that is because you wanted me to get into school earlier. So logically, I am twenty-six,' Arjun takes a big bite while speaking and scrolling through his WhatsApp chats. He turns into a free child with her.

Well, that is common for all these days.

Ignoring his lack of dining etiquette, his mother continues her bombarding, 'Whatever! Does not matter, and even twenty-six is old enough to make out the difference between right and wrong, no?' She looks at him, expecting a few words from him.

He cannot take chances by arguing with her. Therefore, he prefers to give priority to his favourite palak paneer. She repeats before he does a last clean sweep of his plate with his finger.

Arjun knows that her next words would be about selecting a few photographs, knowing more about them and then finalizing one to marry.

Sometimes he wonders, does marriage happen this way?

He is certainly not ready for this.

Arjun has seen his dad following his mother's instructions. His father got married this way. Probably, his mom wants to continue the tradition of dominance.

'Mom, please, not again,' Arjun replies having loads of question in his mind.

'Your friends are getting married. Do you know that?' she insists that he listen to her.

Arjun nods, looking at her, still chewing the last bite, and says, 'I know that but how do you know that?'

Arjun had blocked her on Facebook a month ago because she used to check out girls from his Facebook profile and discuss them at the dinner table with him. However, that didn't work because she knew how to create a new profile.

'Every week at least one or two of your friends are changing their status from 'Single' to 'Married' and if there is any status that says from 'Immature' to 'Mature', you are not even eligible for that. Are you?'

Ved burps out and laughs.

'Mom, again you...' Arjun gets the whole idea why this discussion has even started.

'That's okay Kusum. Let him be a man, a good man for a good girl,' his Nanu says passing by and sipping a glass of warm water.

'That, he will never be,' his mother says.

'That's not fair,' Arjun utters.

'I am your mother and mothers have all the right to check whether you are doing right or wrong.'

'You are like a typical Indian mother,' Arjun looks at her with suspecting eyes. He is trying to think what else she knows about him. Arjun has many secrets, which he has never shared with anyone. He is just worried about the day when she comes to know about them and perhaps disown him. What will be the day when it happens?

'How's it?' she asks ladling more palak paneer into the bowl. Arjun knows if Indian wives and mothers are pampering too much, something is coming up next after the dinner. Trying to divert her mind, he replies instantly, 'It's good as always. I miss your food in Mumbai.'

Appreciation is the best solution to avoid consequences, Arjun knows. Before he finishes the last bite, she asks, pouring water into the glass. 'So you stayed with Anushka for the whole night?'

'What?' Ved says.

'When?' Nanu smiles from the other side of the table. He is the one always in his character to support Arjun. He wants Arjun to propose to Anushka one day, and settle down with her. Maybe Arjun is not ready, and he has not confessed in front of him.

'Mom, I have stayed at her home, that does not mean I have stayed with Anushka. There is a difference between both the phrases,' he tries to explain, as he is always prepared with explanations. Sometimes, explanations are always better than straightforward answers.

'But there was no need to stay; don't you have a home to live? This is so humiliating for me, what will they think about our reputation?' she definitely does not approve, and that is evident from her words.

'I am asking something,' she says. She looks tired. Then

everyone gets up from the dining table. She sets the cover of the sofa and sits on it.

'Mom, I had missed my flight, and Dimpy Aunty told me to stay as I had to book a ticket again. Well, next morning I left early. I didn't even have tea,' Arjun says, sounding innocent. Probably using the last weapon to pause the discussion.

But, has he?

NOT REALLY. Probably that is the reason he is always his mom's target.

'Has Dimpy Aunty given you birth?

'That you must be knowing or maybe Dad,' Arjun tries to crack a joke. He fails.

'And how did you miss your flight? Going to her place, having dinner and staying overnight, what is all this?'

'Okay, sorry, my Lord. Anything else?' Arjun rests his hands on her shoulders, and things are easily diverted.

'You are my respect and pride, don't do anything which makes us look bad in the society,' she says.

'How come you missed your flight?' she asks him again.

'Actually, when you told me about the ceremony, I booked my flight the next minute, but in sleep, I booked a reverse flight.'

'That is why I am saying, find a girl for him and get him married. What about Anushka? She is not that bad,' his Nanu joins the discussion walking towards the centre of the hall.

'Nanu...what does "she is not that bad" mean?'

'You have made him your blue-eyed boy,' she walks away into the kitchen carrying the dishes.

'Have you met her? Why don't you invite her to your sister's wedding?' Nanu grins at him.

'Do you still think it is plausible after seeing her reaction?' Arjun speaks softly so that only Nanu could hear him.

'You invite them, and I will handle the rest. She is your

mother but don't forget I am her father,' Nanu seems like a boss.

'Love you, Nanu.'

Ved enters in a hurry asking, 'Arjun, are you ready?'

'Where are you going?' Arjun's mom asks him. Before she gets any idea about what they are going to do, Arjun replies, 'Nothing, Ved wants to go shopping.'

'Shopping?'

'Yeah, actually, he has some events coming up so he needs my help,' Ved explains to her. He has also come to know that explanations are better than straightforward answers.

Arjun gestures to Nanu to not say anything in front of her.

'When will you be back?' she enquires.

'Before dinner,' Arjun replies and walks into his room, with Ved following him. Arjun looks around hurriedly, but takes time to choose his clothes meticulously. He wears his favourite blue shirt. It sits well on his well-sculpted sporty physique, and he teams it up with a blue blazer.

His mother suspects something is amiss.

Ved leaves the first two buttons of his shirt unbuttoned. He thinks he looks smart and his shoulders seem broader. Boys look good with broad shoulders. Arjun disagrees with his idea and checks himself out on his phone's screen. He looks handsome though Ved calls him a schoolboy.

'Are you sure you are going for shopping?' she enquires again.

'Yes Aunty, we will go shopping, and if we are done on time, then we will go to meet Adrika,' Ved confesses to her.

Arjun looks at him. He does not want to tell her at this time.

'Adrika?' she asks.

'Adrika? Is she here in Mumbai? Can't I come with you?' his Nanu questions and then looks at his mother. Before she says anything, Arjun responds, 'I'll take you some other day, promise.'

Then, they both leave.

Three

THE CIRCLE OF four is incomplete without Adrika.

Ved, Arjun, Adrika and Anushka were in the same college—Anushka was a year senior, while Ved, Arjun and Adrika were classmates. The friendship which was cherished five years ago in college, was going to be renewed now with a lot more trust and love.

They are adults now. However, their notorious acts have not been discussed out of the circle of four. That is the best part about them.

There is a lot to catch up and gossip about.

The A3V group was famous in college because it had every kind of person. While Ved and Anushka were extroverts, Arjun and Adrika were introverts. Arjun, Ved and Anushka had many friends but not Adrika. Her character was very well-wounded, she loved writing letters.

As far as Arjun and Ved know, she still writes letters to her friends and relatives on special occasions. She is well-loved for her determination. She is quite similar to Arjun. Maybe because they share the same zodiac sign.

Adrika had very few friends in college and never liked going out or participating in any extracurricular activities until she met Ved and Anushka who pulled her out from her aloofness.

Ved and Adrika always stood first in their class, Adrika used to be first from the top and Ved from the bottom. She was obsessed with books while he was obsessed with football. They both could never have a conversation on one topic because Ved only knew football, and Adrika was interested in talking about books. Arjun was the link among all because he was obsessed with nothing. He accepted everything—whatever came his way.

Adrika had saved Arjun and Ved many times by testifying for their non-involvement in acts they were completely involved in. She had pretended to be Arjun's mother over phone calls to save him from disciplinary action, Ved's girlfriend when Ved needed couple passes for clubs. *A saviour friend in need is a forever friend indeed.*

She knew their secrets and scandals. Adrika was not just a good friend whom they haven't met for a few years, but she was also their best friend. However, they all celebrated each memorable moment over conference calls. *Few relationships are not defined by time because they grow with the moments we spend with the person, not with time.* They are going to relive those moments again. Adrika has relocated to Mumbai again, to join Cadbury India as a principal chocolate taster.

Meeting an old friend is like reading a favourite book with all your favourite characters. Arjun checks himself in the mirror, his nervousness and excitement evident.

A light stubble shows on his face. He smiles. He has transformed himself over the years. He has begun to look attractive and smart.

He is certain that Adrika will not believe the change in his personality, as they haven't met in a long time.

'What are you up to?' Ved kicks him while trying to set his hair. He has looked into the mirror three times in the last few minutes. Anyone can see the excitement on his face. Ved is equally eager to meet Adrika.

He also has some crazy memories with her. It is true that small memories remain forever.

'Let's go, else Aunty will ask about these bags,' Ved points out at the sweets and shopping bags Arjun's mother had brought for Ved, Arjun and Anushka. Arjun has done his best to make a goody bag for Adrika in this short period.

'I am just being a little conscious about what Adrika would like, or should I get something else for her? It has been more than five years. I wish I still knew her likes and dislikes.'

'Arjun you already have five bags,' says Ved and picks up two bags. He gets ready to leave.

Arjun grins.

Nanu is standing at the door. He stops smiling when Arjun looks at him.

'Nanu, what happened? Please manage things if mom asks anything,' Arjun says.

'Don't worry about that. I can handle your mother,' he hugs him.

'What happened Nanu?'

'Who says you are still immature?' Nanu becomes emotional.

'Mom says,' Arjun jokes.

'You care for everyone you know. Not just your mother, but we all are blessed to have a son like you,' Nanu says. Arjun feels his emotions through the grip of fingers on his shoulder.

'Nanu chill, long way to go,' Arjun makes him smile.

'Yes Nanu, just chill,' Ved adds.

'Deliver my blessings to Adrika,' Nanu tells Ved, and asks Arjun, 'What do you think of Anushka? She is intelligent, social and hot too.'

He winks.

'Yes, I agree with you Nanu,' Ved takes his side.

'She is my college friend,' Arjun looks at both of them.

'Relationships grow like this. I have seen many things in life. I am not forcing you, just telling you as a friend that even a mother takes nine months to grow a baby and make that baby ready to come into the world. How can someone know the person enough in just a few hours or weeks and spend the rest of their life with them? So take your time, if you have someone in your life—either Anushka or anyone, I am there to help you. You know, when I got married, I hadn't even seen your Nani and after marriage, it took time, but she started enjoying my tantrums. We used to argue on the smallest of issues. However, we loved each other more than anything else. We even enjoyed the fights. Life is not as short as we think it is. It has several colours and you have seen only a few. So take your time,' he picks up his glass of buttermilk from the side table and sipping some of the cool drink, asks, 'Do you agree?'

'Yes, I agree. Do you miss Nani a lot?' Arjun asks.

A tear rolls down Nanu's eyes, which he slowly brushes off. 'Yes, I do, but she will not come back,' he places his hand on his forehead.

'Now you should go, you must be getting late,' he adds.

'Nanu, I am guessing you were more romantic than Nani, is it?' Ved jokes.

'Once you are back, I have many stories to tell,' he gives him a funny look.

'Arjun, you could've told me that you are going to meet Adrika,' his mom said.

'I thought you'll shout at me and I really wanted to meet her before she leaves.'

'Why don't you call her home?'

'Here, no. We will be back for dinner or earlier.'

Carrying the bags, Arjun and Ved leave for Adrika's home.

♥

Anushka is already waiting at the doorstep when Ved, with his hands full of three bags, and Arjun reach Adrika's home.

'Cheers to the reunion,' Anushka chirps.

'I never thought the reunion would be like this.'

'Seriously! I never thought,' she repeats. The repetition defines her happiness and excitement.

Arjun notices her wide, stunning smile that has become more prominent over the last couple of years. Anushka looks beautiful. The innocent yet playful expression in her eyes, the pronounced cheekbones and permanent dimple on her chin that Arjun is very attracted to. He would have been obsessed with it if he had one.

Anushka looks elegant. Arjun has always appreciated her long eyelashes, her shiny long honey-coloured hair, luscious red lips and her luminous black eyes; her understated beauty is enough to make many men go weak in their knees. Arjun smiles and gives her a warm hug.

It has been years since they all last met. It always feels special to Arjun whenever Anushka is around. She is the best companion. Things become easier for him with her around.

'You are looking lovely. This dress suits you,' Arjun appreciates her purple dress. 'Thanks. Well, this is called a palazzo,' Anushka corrects him and rings the doorbell. They wait for few seconds before Ved buzzes once more.

The last-minute touch-up is the most important—Arjun sets his hair and licks his lips in anticipation. He does this whenever he is feeling conscious about himself.

Creaking and groaning at the hinges, the door opens. Standing at the door is a small, cute girl. Arjun rechecks the flat number and looks at Ved.

'Is she her daughter?' Ved jokes.

Arjun rings the bell again, ignoring Ved's irrelevant question, expecting Adrika to appear at the door.

'Who's there?' Adrika asks from inside in a loud and clear voice. Arjun does not answer. He wants her to see them first.

Adrika darts across the hall surprised, 'Oh my God.'

Adrika keeps staring at them. She just can't believe her eyes. 'Oh my God. Is it a dream that you all are here?'

Few relationships don't need time to cherish because they are cherished with feelings that have been shared over a period of time. Just as the number of meetings or calls don't define their bond, which is based on the foundation of love and trust.

Her short black hair is bouncing against her back, her sleeves are fluttering and her high heels are clacking against the tiled floor. They synchronize their steps with her and enter the house. Her place is done up beautifully and is very different from other homes they have been to. It is decorated with stickers, posters of cartoon characters, wind chimes and chandeliers, with a chocolatey fragrance all around.

'Are you going somewhere?' asks Anushka.

'No, I just came back,' Adrika responds in a fawning voice.

'A daughter outside wedlock?' Anushka asks pointing at the little girl.

Adrika starts laughing, 'She is my neighbour's daughter. She came over to have chocolates.'

'I thought only Arjun was coming. I still can't believe this,' Adrika says, beaming.

Neither Arjun nor Adrika are able to believe that so much has changed between them in all these years. Many things have changed except the bond that they still share. Adrika approaches and hugs Arjun. They just needed this for a very long time. Moreover, she deserved a long warm hug for what she had gone through in the past few years. Emotions run through her eyes and she drops her head on his shoulder and bursts into tears.

'Hey, don't do that. I have come all the way to make you smile not to cry,' Arjun says into her ears. He holds her for some time.

'Let me...' Adrika replies, her words interrupted by her sniffs.

'Okay, my shoulder remains here,' Arjun says, trying to change her mood.

'Shut up,' she says, sniffing for a while, and then wipes her face. Ved and Anushka reach for them and put their hands on her shoulder.

'Life has changed a lot, Arjun. I miss those days and miss you both so much.'

'I am always with you, Adrika,' Arjun does not want to speak any further because then he too wouldn't be able to stop his tears then.

Their parents think they are still kids, but this meeting redefines the maturity of everyone. How well they understand each other even after years.

Sometimes you can only share things with your friends. Adrika has a lot to say, so Arjun, Anushka and Ved let her speak. Adrika feels the touch of friends that she had needed for a very long time. Their arms feel like the safest place on earth. The relationship among friends is the most beautiful feeling which they are reliving once again.

Arjun runs his fingers through her hair and says, 'It's okay.'

Arjun looks at her while she is trying to hide her tears behind her curls. She wipes her eyes on his shoulder and looks at him.

'Hey, see what we have got for you,' Ved peeps into one of the bags while handing it over to her.

'What's that?'

'Your favourite dress, that you wanted in college days. I know it's not in trend anymore...' Arjun smirks.

Before he could explain, Adrika interrupts him, grinning, and says, 'You still remember that?'

She opens the bag.

'This is so beautiful,' hanging the dress from her shoulders, she continues, 'Now you have encouraged me to diet and wear this as soon as possible.'

Arjun laughs, 'I don't think so. For me, you will always be pretty.'

'Your expectation will definitely ruin me,' Adrika says laughing.

'You haven't changed except putting on some extra kilos,' says Ved, pulling her legs.

'Shut up, I still look better than you,' she teases him back.

'Yes, yes, I know how many crushes you had in college,' Ved says, reminiscing the time they spent together in college.

'And what if we discuss your washroom kisses and other stories?' Adrika takes control of the conversation. Ved goes silent.

Arjun and Anushka laugh.

'Okay, okay. We should not discuss all this in front of a kid,' Ved doesn't have a thing to say. The little girl runs away to the other room.

'This man got many things for you,' Ved adds sitting on the sofa. Others also settle down.

'He had to. He owes me many things,' Adrika says, happily taking all the bags from his hand and keeping them on the table.

'So how's everyone and what's new?' she asks, pushing her curls behind her ear.

'Everyone is well at home,' says Arjun.

Ved adds, 'Aunty is desperately trying to find a girl for him.'

She giggles, 'I know, she had called me to know if there is someone in his life. She has become so much possessive about you, Arjun. Why don't you settle down?' Adrika says looking at Anushka and Arjun.

'Chill! Chill! I am just twenty-six. There is enough time for that. We have many more exciting things to discuss.'

'When did you come here? You have made a beautiful home,' Anushka looks appreciatively around the room.

'Thanks, I just came two days back. I wanted to settle things before inviting you guys over,' she simpers in a dry voice but looks very happy seeing them.

The house looks contemporary and spread a lot of positivity.

'So the girl has become more annoying and workaholic, is it?' Ved pops up in between before the conversation could go in any other direction. Adrika laughs, placing her hand on her rosy lips and curling a strand of hair around her finger.

'So...how do you manage everything? You wake up early in the morning, get ready to go to the office, work till late at night, go back and then plan for the next day?' Anushka asks, pulling a chair and sitting near a table, which is piled up with papers and files and a few chocolate baskets. Everyone could smell coffee in every corner of her house.

'Yes, that's what I do,' she smiles.

'You are crazy about chocolates, isn't it?' Arjun asks.

'That is my bread and butter,' she says laughing. 'You all must be hungry. Should I make something for you?'

'No, Arjun will make his famous Maggi and relive those moments again,' Ved says, and Adrika interrupts, 'Yes, yes. And I used to jump my hostel's walls along with my roommates just to get one bite of it.'

'That is a great idea,' Anushka looks enthusiastic.

'I have a bottle of wine as well,' Adrika sounds like she is in a mood to party.

'Should I help you with something?' Anushka asks Arjun.

'No, no. You girls sit and gossip. It has a been long time,' Arjun says and goes into the kitchen.

'You both must have many things to gossip about. Carry on.'

Ved follows Arjun into the kitchen.

♥

After having delicious bowls of Maggi and a few glasses of wine, it was time for everyone to leave after making promises to keep in touch and meet soon. Ved hands over the car keys to Arjun as they began preparing for their departure.

'You guys sit comfortably, I'll drive today,' Anushka says, taking the keys from Arjun and getting inside the car.

'Okay, all yours,' Arjun smiles.

They all wave at Adrika, who is standing near the car.

Arjun peeps out of the window and looks at Adrika. He waves once more, assuring her that he is always there for her.

♥

'What's that?' Ved enquires from the back seat when Arjun gives a diary to Anushka who is driving.

'Nothing,' says Arjun before Anushka could say anything.

'Show me,' Ved repeats.

'Is that the same notebook you were asking Adrika about?' Ved is now curious. If it was a personal notebook of Adrika's, then why had she given it to him when there had been so many arguments on it earlier. Ved knows that she has never shared it with anybody.

Arjun smiles.

'What? Why are you smiling?' probes Ved.

'She gave it to you finally,' Ved interrogates him and then

looks at Anushka, waiting for her to say something.

'No she didn't. I found it on her table.'

'What the fuck! That is why you called Anushka into the room that time?'

'Arjun I told you, that is not right. At least you could ask her before taking her things,' Anushka now regretted doing it.

She endures, 'He took it without her permission. I told him not to, but he didn't listen to me.'

'I wanted this. I had asked Adrika several times for it, but she always gave stupid reasons not to share,' Arjun says without any regret.

'So you'll steal things?' Ved questions. He is disappointed with Arjun. He had not expected this from him.

'I think we should go back and return it to her,' Anushka is being ethically correct. However, sometimes you don't need to be morally right for some good reasons, Arjun believes.

'It's not right, but it's okay,' Arjun smiles and continues, 'Let's go, Mom must be waiting for us. She has called thrice already.'

'And no more discussion about this,' Arjun points at the notebook and wraps it in his arms as if he does not want to give it to anybody.

'You are coming with us?' Ved asks Anushka.

'No, I'll take a cab from there to my home,' Anushka replies.

'Why don't you join us for dinner? Nanu also wanted to meet you. Tell Aunty that you are having dinner with friends,' says Ved looking at Arjun for agreement.

'That is not the problem. Probably some other day,' she smiles.

'Well, I wish I could read this,' she adds, pointing out to the notebook. Anushka is eager to know why Arjun has taken it without Adrika's permission. There must be something in it.

'Okay. Done,' Arjun says.

'Then let's not go home,' Anushka says. She wants to live her life exactly as everyone does with friends—no fear, no worries and they would manage things if anything goes wrong. She can blame them for no reason.

'Let's go to the beach,' Arjun proposes, the weather is nice.

'That's what I was thinking about,' Anushka replies.

Arjun asks to stop the car by the roadside and informs his mom that he will have dinner with Ved and Anushka. A U-turn takes them to Bandstand in half an hour. Then suddenly. . .

Four

THE SKY IS cloudy and dark. It is always so in the evening. The sea, inadvertently, becomes a passive listener for all. This is the place where Arjun has so many memories. This is the place which has a lot of significance for Ved, Arjun and Anushka.

Even before Ved can get out of the car and check out some girls passing by, it begins to rain.

'Oh fuck.'

This is not what he had expected after coming such a long way in hopes of listening to a stolen story and spending some good time in due course by the seaside.

Arjun switches on the light. Being a weekend, the beach is crowded. People are enjoying the weather, relaxing and spending time with their loved ones. For some, rains don't really matter.

'What do we do now?' Anushka asks Arjun, looking at him and thinking that he has all the answers. There is always a Superman among friends, who always has a solution for everything.

'Do you know about Section 378 under IPC?' Ved giggles.

'I haven't stolen anything. I'll tell her soon,' Arjun says solemnly. Logically, he can be booked under Section 378—theft under Indian Panel Code. Ved and Anushka burst out laughing but settle down quickly. Suddenly, Anushka's phone rings and she picks it up, moving her head in the corner while Ved and Arjun have a conversation. Arjun ignores her. Anushka disconnects the call.

'Don't make me feel like I have committed a crime,' Arjun pulls out the notebook from under his right shoulder. They catch a whiff of his cologne. It smells fresh and masculine. Not overwhelming, but rather refreshing. The sleek leather interior, with ocean air freshener turns the car into an old library.

'Nothing can be more comfortable than this back seat,' Anushka gets comfortable.

'You got it.'

'Well, Nanu is coming in a minute,' Anushka tells Arjun and Ved.

'How come?'

'He wanted to speak to me, so I called him. He is reaching soon in a cab,' Anushka explains.

'You guys cook a different story altogether,' says Arjun.

Words dissolve in the opening of the notebook. There is perfect silence, a sensational fragrance and just their breathing. And then Nanu arrives.

They find themselves in the pages of that old notebook and share with Nanu the story they had started in college a few years ago.

♥

A Few Years Ago

Adrika is from Lucknow and has dreams that every Indian girl has. Her childhood wasn't as good as her other friends'. That is the reason she has always been an introvert. Our childhood plays a vital role in what we become in future.

Not just school education, but observing your parents also influences your childhood. We learn more from parents than books. She hasn't been that happy seeing her mother taking care of everyone and still being humiliated by her own family.

Growing up, she saw her father working hard even after office hours. Due to the lack of a convent education because of financial issues, Adrika had completed her schooling from a very ordinary school. Seeing her neighbours' kids playing video games and going on picnics, not for a moment did she feel sad because her father always told her that life is not as short as we think, it's long and we can change it, learn from it and again change it according to our acts and hard work. The values she received from her father during their morning walks or at the dinner table helped in shaping her life. She began dreaming of a better life. Her neighbours would tell her father not to send her out of the town for higher education. They said, 'Girls go out of control if they move away from their parents.'

However, taking all the criticism in his stride, her father let her do what she wanted. When she started college, he even asked if she liked someone in college. Though there had always been a tradition of arranged marriage in her family, he had given her that space to decide about her life and career. He had always told Adrika not to listen to others, to just do what she feels good and best for her life. 'We only get one life,' he would say, adding, 'It is the age when we transform from teenager to a man or a woman.'

We become the person we transform to. He just had one girl to make his dreams come true. Today, he must be smiling looking at her somewhere from the sky. He is a part of the galaxy now.

Her father had a small candle making business. He died when Adrika started her first year of college. She lost one of the biggest foundations on which she built her dreams. She had become lonely. Adrika wanted to stay back at home and take care of her mother. However, her mother supported her and told her to take an education loan and continue her studies. Dropping from college would break the dreams that his father saw in his eyes.

Those were tough days for her, but she managed to move on and build her career day-by-day. We think others' lives are better because we never know the situation they go through. Everyone has struggles in life.

♥

Girls are always closer to their fathers. When her father passed away, Adrika became isolated. When we are lonely, we start searching for voices in that loneliness. She found one.

There was someone in the initial days of college who had a crush on her. She was never ready for any relationship, having friends like Ved, Anushka and a person like Arjun. However, she never expected that he would propose to her so soon. We all become weak in love and affection. Though taking a few months, she realized she had found the right one for her. She was on top of the world, but somewhere she was afraid too because she had seen her friends left heartbroken over failed relationships. It's a dream of every girl to find someone who loves her more than anything. She had one in her life now. He was there whenever she needed him. They started going out for overnight trips. That means a lot. Even a kiss does. When a girl does it, it says she has accepted that person from her heart. When a guy does it, it means he can fight for her no matter what the situation is in life.

However, her life turned upside down after a year, when he started shouting and abusing her during small arguments. She lost her self-respect in the relationship. Though she was with him, she wasn't happy because respect and trust are all that you expect in a relationship. If you lose it, you lose everything, and there is no relationship. She was always questioned about the things she tried to fix, but nothing worked out. Sometimes we do wrong things to save a relationship that means everything to us, but nobody looks at the right side.

He left her when she had become dependent on him.

When we fall in love, everything looks amazing, but life always has another side to it. She went through a tragic heartbreak just after few months of her relationship. Her perception of love had changed after that. Life changes herself after being in a relationship, she had realized. She felt isolated after losing her father and going through a failed relationship, but this time with more tears and awful memories. She started hating her own body parts wherever she was touched. This relationship was a nightmare for her that she never wanted to discuss with anyone. She had come to know the reality of it. She stopped talking to everyone. She spent all her time into studies after a few months of depression. That tragic incident turned her into an introvert—forever.

Five

IT'S NOT ALWAYS true that opposites attract. Sometimes, people with similar sense of humour, or two mischievous people can easily understand each other.

Over a period of time, the bond among Adrika, Ved, and Arjun has become stronger. In the last year of college, they miss Anushka in their gang as being a year senior to them she has already started working in Mumbai, and is calling them there once they finish college.

Arjun has been a problem-solver in Adrika's life. She can feel and see the change in herself over time. She had later joined the college youth club where she spent most of her time. It is there that she met Ved and Iona through Arjun. They all became friends.

Iona is Adrika's best friend. An easygoing person, she is social, responsible and passionate about her future. Iona is coping with last year of college, but she is an avid traveller. She is poised, spontaneous and outgoing. Her dream is to travel the whole world some day. Iona is a hipster by heart and very fashion-conscious.

Adrika, on the other hand, is never worried about what she has to wear, and she buys clothes when Iona is around because they wear the same size. Nevertheless, Adrika has to cope with wearing Iona's funky shirts with swear words printed on it. Being so opposite, how they ended up becoming such close friends is anyone's guess.

Ved and Iona would pray to not get seats in the front in the examination hall, and Adrika and Arjun are always worried about the question paper—what if something comes out of syllabus. Gosh! They are not just trouble for their friends but also for neighbours in the examination hall because they never share their answers with anyone. Probably others think they are self-obsessed creatures.

However, Arjun always sits in the front row with Adrika during the lectures. Adrika never understands this logic, but they know every question the professor asks will be aimed at people seated in the last row, who are different in nature. Only one thing is common for all—the bond of friendship.

It is a Saturday morning when Adrika rolls in her bed and shrinks back again. She longs to sleep for some time after an impulsive night out. She feels sluggish. She closes her eyes for some time, and when she finally gets up, the tableside grandfather clock reads 9 a.m. It runs faster when you want to nap for just a minute more—the universal fact.

Sometimes she misses home because at home, her mother is a pre-alarm who starts waking her up an hour before she actually has to get up. It so happens, when we get more freedom, we start missing restrictions of our own.

Yesterday, it was just an idea to skip boozing in the hostel and go out with friends for a night out, instead. However, later Adrika and her friends finished the full bottle of vodka that Iona had kept hidden in her cubbyhole from her roommates. Iona had left it under her surveillance, but Adrika believes that every bottle is destined to be finished by particular people. Iona missed the bottle, and Adrika missed Iona during the night out.

This was the first night out without Iona. Adrika has to pay for this indulgence.

Adrika looks at the bottle that rolls out from a gust of wind. It still has a few drops in it. She notices a few cigarette butts that her neighbours have thrown in the balcony. She hates them. She tries to focus her sight on the message, 'Smoking is injurious to health' written on the cigarette box. We usually notice little things when we are alone.

♥

Do everything in life once in a while to know the good and bad side of it. She has heard that lesson from Iona. Adrika has rarely had alcohol before and if she has had it, then only with Iona and Ved. However, last night, some hostel friends had all the reasons to party. A toast to Adrika for all that she has achieved in her life. Despite being an engineer, she has chosen an exciting career of a chocolate taster.

Yesterday, she even smoked flavoured hookah and enjoyed making rings in the air. Adrika did twenty-seven in a row. She is excited to share the incident with Iona once she comes back from her vacation.

Adrika had craved to postpone the plan as Iona was on an extended vacation after the internal exams. She was supposed to come back last week. She has taken a few extra days' leave as everyone does. She may reach the hostel anytime today. Adrika hasn't called her yet and is desperately waiting for her to give the most awaited news. Adrika is the first and the luckiest girl in the history of college, who has bagged the coolest job and that too a month before college officially gets over—as an associate chocolate taster in a multinational company.

Isn't it cool? She will start earning even before her college gets over. Life could not get better than this for her. She has to eat chocolates, and she will be paid for it.

Does this job really exist?

Yes, she has already cracked it.

She believes that it is not just about eating chocolates. It's about the fragrance which creates temptation in the human brain and seduces the brain cells to enjoy till it lasts. That is the reason why chocolate-flavoured condoms are more sellable than others. She has given the same answer in the interview. As of now, only one thought is making her conscious—her well-maintained figure.

Adrika is happy now, as she always wanted to do something different in her life. She always believed in hard work and kept the last words of her father in her mind, that life is just about experiences.

Adrika needs to clean the room before someone knocks at the door. Drinking and smoking are strictly prohibited in hostels.

Standing on the balcony, she looks out and imagines her life after months or a year. She is going to be a part of one of the most exciting workplaces.

The weather is a little chilly outside. Wrapping her arms with her hands, Adrika tries to have a look at Iona's balcony which is just a floor above hers. Despite being best friends, Iona and Adrika have decided not to share a room because Adrika never likes Iona's friends, especially those who smoke weed in her room half of the day and for the rest of the day, they just sleep. Because they know that they will get the notes from Iona written by Adrika even if they sleep through the whole semester.

Six

IONA IS EFFICIENT and optimistic. She always tells Adrika that life is mischievous but amazing at the same time; it gives a jerk and pushes back before it takes off to fly high. Iona is right. Life has a quota of both happiness and sadness. If you shed tears initially, later, you will only be left with joy. Life is like that. Therefore, there are amazing things lined up for Adrika. Getting this fantastic job is maybe one of them, but Adrika hasn't told her about it yet. Iona motivates her in all ways she can though her way of motivation is a little different from others.

As Adrika is lazily stretching her body a few drops of water from Iona's balcony fall on her forehead. She raises her neck a little and tries to see into her balcony. She guesses that Iona's roommate has given a bath to the little pug that she has brought in last week. Keeping pets is not allowed in the hostel, but everything seems possible if Iona wants it. For more than half the day, Iona keeps him in Adrika's room. She is sure that nobody will check her room. Safe and secure from all unethical activities.

'What happened Adrika? Planning to jump?' Iona shouts.

'What are you investigating? Ved?' Iona laughs in her balcony, craning her neck to see Adrika.

'You are back?' Adrika cheerfully asks, stretching her neck to see Iona.

'Yes my love,' Iona winks.

'Well, that needs guts,' Adrika adds.

'What does?' Iona asks.

'To call your boy into the girls' hostel,' she almost shouts. It hurts her throat. Maybe because of all the boozing and smoking hookah in the night. Seven glasses are not less. She gets rashes when she crosses four. That's her limit.

'Oh I see, by the way, Ved just left,' Iona takes her head out and smiles at her.

Love had blossomed between Ved and Iona very dramatically a year before. Ved proposed to Iona on her birthday in the academic block in front of Anushka and Arjun while Adrika was busy with her books. Many boys were after Iona, but she chose Ved. They were madly in love.

'What? He was here in your room?' Adrika can't believe Iona has done that.

'You did that?' Adrika asks her, seeking confirmation.

Iona blushes. She looks innocent when she blushes. She continues, 'He wanted to spend time with me, so I called him. We spent a good time.' The last two words signify everything.

Iona looks gracious and admits that nothing happened last night. They must have had sex because the last time when Adrika had opened the cupboard in her room, she had found two strips of condoms and chocolate body paint. Adrika will probably revisit her room and solve the case in a minute. She goes into a wild imaginative reverie for a while and is pulled back to reality when Iona says, 'Now, don't discuss this with Arjun...please.' She knows that Adrika discusses everything with him. Adrika nods and smiles. However, she looks worried.

'Iona, this year we have to appear for placement interviews, don't do anything stupid,' she is still not sure how Ved entered the hostel, climbed the stairs to Iona's fifth-floor room and slept with her. The whole night. Adrika sometimes does not like Iona because of her daring acts. She might discuss this with Ved, tell him that he should concentrate on his studies and get a decent job.

'Don't worry, you have cracked it, and you have the coolest job now,' Iona says sarcastically. She is angry at her that she hasn't told her yet about it.

'You know that? Who told you?' Adrika asks.

'I know. I wanted to hear it from you, but you didn't call,' she retorts.

'I know,' Adrika smiles.

'Listen! Do you have biscuits? Ved finished the whole packet last night and now, what will he eat?' Iona takes her pug out of her balcony, hanging it in the air.

'The whole night, you guys just ate biscuits,' Adrika giggles. 'Poor you guys.'

'Wait, I am coming to your room...' Iona says.

♥

Sometimes, Adrika wishes she could have a life like Iona. Then she recalls what her father had said, 'The grass is always greener on the other side.'

She hears knocking at the door. This must be Iona, she presumes.

'Wait, coming.'

She hides the bottle of vodka behind the dustbin. She takes a minute to pretend that she was busy doing something. Iona catches her so easily. Best friends always do. Therefore, she needs to be alert once she is in the room.

'Are you masturbating?' Iona says, knocking at the door harder.

'Opening baba...opening.'

Before Iona showers her with more such words, she

opens the door and turns back to check whether she has kept everything back in the drawer.

Talking loudly, Iona walks in, carrying the pug in her hands like a baby. She glances around, and in the same high pitch, says, 'I have been knocking for so long.'

'It seems like you are feeding it,' Adrika laughs at her, closing the door and changing the topic.

'My son would wear nappies at least. He pissed on my bed last night,' she makes a face in annoyance.

'Then why did you bring him up here? Well, did he piss or someone else made your bed wet?' Adrika pulls her legs.

'You don't talk to me,' Iona says in disappointment looking around the room. Adrika is hiding something. Iona drops the puppy on the floor.

'What is that?' Iona asks pointing at a bag. She can't resist taking it from Adrika's hands.

'Wait, hold on, it's for you only,' Adrika hands her the bag, 'This is for you and I'll take my love to a special night out,' Adrika hangs on her shoulder.

'Oh my God!' Iona loves the present—a beautiful red dress with a black cardigan that she always wanted to buy and Adrika had promised to get it for her once she got a job.

'Here it goes.'

'Thanks so much. You kept your promise.'

They both laugh.

Over the years, they have become like soul siblings. They go shopping together but buy only one dress, as they both love sharing things with each other. For them, happiness is about sharing feelings, things and moments. They have many problems, but they find a common solution to resolve them. Both are sisters and mothers for each other. Their opinions and perspectives are different, but they give priority to their similarities. For others, they may be just friends. But they are the best of friends.

'What about my party?' Iona is not done yet, 'I told you to wait for me.' She acts pricey.

'It must be costly…' Iona knows her financial situation. Few gifts become precious and priceless when emotions embroider them.

'I am going to be super rich now,' Adrika winks at her. Perhaps she does not want to discuss that.

'My girl is going to be the richest and just by tasting chocolates!' Iona pokes her in her stomach.

'Thanks for the present,' Iona gives her a big hug.

'Everything is changing so fast,' Adrika says.

'Everything will be as great as you wished for,' Iona says. They sit down together.

Adrika opens a packet of biscuits, and Iona picks one. Adrika give a few to the little pug.

'Well, when are you going to stop this babysitting?' Adrika laughs, and Iona joins her.

'When Ved becomes the father of my kid.'

They both laugh.

'It's full-time entertainment for my roommates. They will take care of it. If we get caught, we will give it to Vice Chancellor Maruthhur Gopalamenon Ramachandran (MGR) to play with,' says Iona, who is always making a plan for the VC. She does not like him as she has been caught many times while breaking the rules in college.

'I hope you do not get caught for keeping this,' Adrika warns her.

♥

VC Maruthhur Gopalamenon Ramachandran is the head of the youth club. As complex as his name, he has always given a tough time to Adrika because she has to fill forms on his behalf to get funds for club activities. So, most of the forms are signed off as MGR—short and straightforward. Another reason why Adrika and Iona don't like him is because of the strange sounds he produces while coughing. However, he is proud that Adrika is representing her last college fest—AVIA—this year. AVIA means 'God is my father'. Adrika has chosen the name of the fest this time. The name itself is very close to her life.

As Adrika and Iona are also the coordinators of the Youth Club, the next few days are going to be very exciting yet tiring for all. It's not easy to be a part of the Youth Club. Although it's the best way to take unplanned leaves from classes during the fest and other events, it's also a good opportunity to learn management skills. This year Iona is organizing a fashion show called Panache. Moreover, Adrika wants to end her college journey happily with more excitement and passion by managing all the events.

Seven

WAKING UP NEXT morning, Adrika takes her head out of the cozy blanket and scrolls down the checklist on her phone. Along with Iona, she is managing the fashion show and she has to oversee the final touches to the stage today. The day is going to be hectic.

With eyes wide open, she thinks about the appreciation she has received from everyone on her management skills, even MGR, who always has a problem letting her skip class for Club activities.

'You have done excellent work in the last two weeks, and I hope you finish it that way. Get up Adrika, we are getting late,' Iona says walking into her room. She has a toothbrush in her mouth and a towel is hanging from her shoulders. That is a good morning.

Having a roommate has some advantages and some disadvantages. Well, sometimes it's of course better to be alone and talking to walls rather than listening to her midnight sexual conversations with Ved. Adrika has shifted to Iona's room for a week so that Iona can wake her up on time.

'All's well that ends well,' Iona twitters into her ears.

Adrika is still stretching her body in sluggishness.

'Okay. That, I know. Just five more minutes, let me sleep Iona.' She rolls in bed for some time.

The tableside clock ticks gracefully. Iona is good in analytical skills. She is calculating the schedule.

'I am going to take a shower, so get up and get ready,' Iona says and leaves the room.

♥

Adrika doesn't get up, she continues to roll in bed thinking about her life in just a few months. She does not seem to be in a mood to get up. She spent the whole night preparing charts for the stage.

'Who is it?' looking at the door with tired eyes, asks Adrika as someone knocks at the door.

'Hey it's me, the door got locked from inside,' someone thunders from outside, and the door handle clinks. It is Iona on the other side.

'Hey you lazy ass, it's me,' the irritation in her voice clearly cuts through the door. She makes a guess that Iona would be shivering outside.

'Hey, coming,' she replies releasing herself from the blanket and rushing to open the door before Iona starts abusing her from the other side.

'You are a lazy ass, get ready, and we need to leave now. Ved has called several times,' Iona says authoritatively.

Adrika manages to take a walk to the balcony and comes back. Iona goes to her cupboard to take back her jacket from there that Adrika was wearing last night.

'Sorry I was tired,' Adrika says before Iona says anything about her favourite grey jacket. She is obsessed with it. Probably, it's a gift from Ved.

'That's okay, at least you kept it in the cupboard,' Iona says fitting the jacket on her toned body. Some friends flip you in the air, not to hurt you but to make you fly higher and higher. No matter how and why but they are always with you whenever you need them. Iona is one of them for Adrika.

Iona has a pale complexion with jet-black hair and black eyes. She has a fresh, youthful face and an innocent appeal. She is beautiful, attractive and alluring. She does not wear much make-up, if any at all, and usually wears jeans in college. She loves to wear skirts, but that is not allowed in college. She has to wait for a few months for that until she completes college. She classifies herself as a 't-shirt and Converse shoes' type of girl.

'You are growing so fast Iona. You should say thanks to Ved,' Adrika spanks her ass.

'Get lost and get ready,' Iona says.

Being practical and running short of time, Adrika gives bathing a second priority. Facewash and Iona's perfume are all she needs right now.

While Iona finishes half a packet of chips, Adrika gets ready in a minute.

'Fuck,' Iona shouts suddenly.

'Where and when?' Adrika teases her and takes the packet from her.

'Ved called because it is his inaugural football match today,' Iona finds several missed calls. She begins sending WhatsApp messages to Arjun and Ved and waits for them to get delivered. She keeps staring at the notification check. Ved must be expecting them at the match. He needs encouragement from his best friends. Everyone needs that, and as usual, they won't reach on time. Ved is right in saying, 'Never trust that friend who says, "Hey I'll just come in two minutes."'

'9 a.m., right?' Adrika recalls now, it slipped from her mind due to the fest preparations.

'Yes. I couldn't arrange the costumes and make-up. I haven't finalized the sequence of songs as per the theme for Panache. What to do now?' Iona asks in nervousness.

'Don't worry; we will manage that. Right now, Ved's match is important. Let's break the myth by reaching on time,' Adrika smiles and puts a hand on her shoulder.

'But...'

'We will see to that after the match,' she retorts like a coach and continues, 'Now, let me be a little philosophical. If we can't live the moments for our best friends, there is no use of making others happy by decorating things, isn't it?' Adrika chuckles.

Iona smirks. That must be the reason why everyone loves Adrika. She is not just brilliant in studies, but also knows the value and importance of people around her. Our own situations make us better.

'You have also grown up,' Iona jokes.

'Yes, mentally, and you, physically, as I said.'

Iona abuses her with slangs.

'Do not worry, I have told the juniors to check on the things,' Adrika says and they leave together for the football ground.

♥

Ved is representing his college's football team for the first time. They have already won the knockout match and he is pumped up for the final game now.

Even though he does not expect Iona to reach on time, as usual, but he secretly hopes that his friends come and support him. He needs their wishes because this match is not about winning or losing, it is about the reputation of their college, which was the host this year. The presence of his friends matter to him. As Ved gets ready for a warm-up session on the ground, Iona and Adrika enter the venue, jostling their way through the crowds to get some seats at the deck nearest to the ground.

Ved is wearing a white jersey and shorts, cutting a handsome figure. The match begins; he is just whiling away the time by making his opponent run behind him because they are already leading with 1-0. Suddenly, the opponent reaches the goalpost and shoots a firing goal. Ved misses it. Iona keeps cheering loudly in anticipation of a goal from Ved but it seems that it is not his day. He misses another one.

'He really needs a good coach,' Iona says in disappointment.

'It's okay, and this is his first match. I am happy that he is representing the college,' Adrika, ever the optimistic, says. She is still cheering Ved though his team has lost by 1-2. That is what her friendship is for everyone, that is what makes her special.

Ved walks out of the ground, sweating and panting. He could at least have passed the ball to others closer to the goalpost. He wasn't even giving a pass to others. Now, he could recall his mistakes during the match that he could've avoided and scored an opening goal for his team. Well, it's not a one-man game, and everyone should be responsible for the loss.

'Well played, my boy,' Adrika pats Ved on his back.

'Nothing worked today,' Ved sits on the ground. Adrika gives him the water bottle. Ved can see Arjun approaching them. Ved shouts at him, 'I lost again buddy.'

'That I knew before the match,' Arjun laughs and gives him a high five and continues, 'It's okay, chill! I am sure you played well.' Arjun looks at others.

'Yes, he lost the game but it was the tough one for them,' Adrika expresses. Friends never make you feel like a loser even when you lose.

Iona takes her cell phone out and clicks a 'groupfie' of all of them and posts it on Instagram captioning, 'The best losers.'

'Let's go guys. Close your shops and help us finish our work,' Iona pulls Ved and others follow.

While they are walking towards the stage, Adrika says,

'Arjun! I need your help in understanding the notice from the bank I got in the morning. They have mentioned some excessive amount of the loan.'

'Show the message to me once you are free. By the way, mom has congratulated you. She was so happy for you that you got that job,' Arjun says.

'Thanks for helping me out Arjun.'

Arjun sees Sumrit running behind Ved.

'Hey mate!' Sumrit shouts.

Ved and Iona turn around. Tired but happy. He responds, 'Hi buddy, congratulations! You played really well.'

Sumrit is the captain of the winning football team. His positive nature makes him everyone's favourite. His team had lifted him up the moment the referee whistled.

There are rumours around that after college he is going to join a prestigious management college whose interview he has cleared.

He is one of those who follow the 'first engineering and then MBA' route and then settle down.

Sometimes, Sumrit feels that he should not give a damn about his MBA, that he should just leave everything and concentrate only on football. He really plays well and if he continues, he can surely do miracles. The next moment he is not so sure if he will do well as a player in the end. Hard work in sports only looks good in movies. He knows there is no scope of football in India. He is confident about his game, but he is worried about the lack of opportunities and exposure in the field of sports in general. Hence, the MBA seems to be a concrete, safe plan. Maybe he is being more practical. Perception varies from person to person.

'Thanks! I wanted to congratulate you too, the team you lead and the team I lead is a different issue,' Sumrit says, settling down and inhaling the fresh air, 'I really liked the way you lead your team. I just had a thought if you don't mind...'

Meanwhile, Arjun and Adrika also reach the spot and the girls get busy with the stage arrangements for the most awaited evening of the year.

'Thanks! Yes, sure. I should listen to the winning captain,' Ved gives him a playful punch in his stomach.

'Why don't we all collaborate and play for the same team? We should represent the university for the next match. We are anyway three colleges under the same university. Management will also not have any problem,' Sumrit explains.

Arjun moves a step forward and congratulates Sumrit, 'It's an excellent plan but Ved should think about the collaboration. It's an injustice to all those players who are working hard to play for this team.'

Ved adds, 'Also, only eleven players can play not twenty-two. I do not mean to offend you but it just about my other players...'

'I agree with you...I believe you have a good team and are a wonderful captain,' Sumrit wishes him luck and makes way to the faculty guest house.

'See you at DJ night, Sumrit,' Ved says, and Sumrit waves in acceptance.

♥

'How much time do they take? We got ready in less than ten minutes,' Ved says, walking by the entry gate of their hostel.

Arjun has chosen his clothes diligently because he has some surprises planned. He has chosen to wear his favourite white cotton shirt with a blazer. He closes the top button of his shirt—an effect which gives a little peek at his well-built, muscular chest, giving him a rugged look. He does not forget to carry a muffler these days and that makes him look cute. He has started carrying it from the day Iona and Ved told him that he looks more attractive with it. Everything fits his sculpted body. Men look attractive with their attitude, just like the way girls carry grace on their face. Everyone looks so decent and elegant.

'Because you can't wear backless,' Arjun points towards Iona, who is walking out of the gate.

Iona is dressed in a backless dress. It fits her toned body perfectly. She looks spectacular. Adrika also looks fabulous in a two-piece dress with a pair of small fish-shaped earrings that Arjun has gifted her a few weeks ago on her birthday, with small diamonds on it. Adrika and Iona have managed everything perfectly.

'How am I looking?' Ved asks Arjun.

'You don't need any description today. Everyone knows you after today's match.'

'The one I lost,' Ved says in sarcasm.

'I didn't say that,' Arjun keeps one hand on his shoulder, 'Chill! Now don't go into depression.'

They reach the stage from the back. It looks magnificent. With a capacity to accommodate more than a thousand people; there are huge speakers, just ready to make everyone go crazy. There is a thin wall just to keep the girls separated from the boys, but it won't last long once the DJ starts.

Iona and Adrika look happy and satisfied. Their hard work has paid off.

'You guys have just nailed it,' Arjun says.

'Yayy! We did it.' Iona is happy. As Adrika steps around to find Ved, her phone flashes the arrival of a new message on WhatsApp. She taps it. It is from Sumrit. She swipes and ignores it, thinking she will respond after the party.

'Where is Ved?' Adrika asks Arjun.

'I don't know. He was just here.'

Adrika calls him and then...

♥

An announcement: 'Hi everyone, may I have your few minutes?'

It is Ved. He looks taller on the dais and broad-shouldered, with a mop of dark hair and heavy, solemn brows that are offset by a boyish grin. His black eyes gleam behind square-framed glasses that keep slipping down his long nose. He is wearing a grey U-shaped waistcoat.

'What the hell is he doing on the stage?' Iona asks. Arjun and Adrika are also surprised.

'Is he drunk?' Arjun enquires.

'And when did he start wearing glasses?' Adrika asks.

'The new look,' says Arjun, concentrating on his words.

'He is looking good,' Adrika adds.

'Was he supposed to do anything?' Iona checks with Adrika.

'I have no idea, what is he doing there?' Adrika replies, still trying to figure out what he is doing on the stage.

'Hey Arjun, Iona, Adrika,' Ved says over the mic. Loud and clear. They reach near the stage.

'Hi everyone, please settle down. I know, it's not a part of the plan today, but I won't take much time of yours. My name is Ved; a few of you probably know me as I lost the match today.' He gives Sumrit a thumbs-up. He applauds in response. Ved continues, 'and those who don't know me, my name is Ved Gulati. I consider this as my farewell speech so please don't take any disciplinary action against me.' He smiles looking at the faculty sitting in the front row.

He continues, 'This is the last year of our college, and we

all are being placed in good companies. Many congratulations to you all. I just wanted to take this opportunity to raise a toast to one of my friends. My wishes to her,' Ved points out to Adrika. She smiles back, and Arjun and Iona hug her. The happiness is visible on her face.

'Soon we all will be going to different cities, different places. Things will change. Sometimes we will have time, but for most of the time it will get difficult to take out time from our busy schedules to call old friends. The acts, the plays, the songs we do here, will just remain in our memories. Life will be changed, trust me. I have seen my seniors whom I helped to complete their assignments, and now they have disappeared. I am just afraid to finish college so soon.'

Everyone giggles.

'Well, that was necessary. Probably that is the phase of life. However, there are certain things, which are not in our hands and intentionally we don't want to write wrong answers in examination.'

More giggles.

'Friends are like a seesaw. When we are low and go down, a friend pushes us to reach higher. They keep all their wishes hidden from us just to make us feel happy and comfortable. They fight. But we never see them loving us as we want them, but they do. They do cry for us. They laugh to make us laugh. There is no species in the world who party when their friends lose. They do. They appreciate when we lose. Their dictionary is different. That does not have anything which discourages us. We all have those friends. So now the time is to go on to the other side of the swing, and take them higher with all your hard work, love and success, and don't forget them even after years. When we feel low in life, just take some time out from the busy schedule and just call an old friend. I promise, that will be one of the best moments in life. Thank you!

'Welcome to AVIA,' Ved says and a big screen flashes on the background.

'Well, AVIA does not only stand for dedication, but these initials also signify our four friends—Arjun, Ved, Iona, Adrika. So, enjoy your awesome life with your wonderful friends. Sorry Arjun, for stealing your speech but I think that is what we all do as friends,' Ved gives Arjun a frown. Adrika has become emotional. Ved steps down and everyone applauds. Ved has said enough in a short speech.

'Dude, I missed few of the words as I couldn't read it well,' Ved says. Arjun replies, 'Chill! It was superb.'

'Oh, you are crying,' Iona hugs Adrika.

'No, no. I am okay.'

♥

Suddenly music fills the arena and all they can see are dancing bodies tangled together. There are multicoloured flashing lights near the dance floor, but they are not bright enough to reach beyond that. It is going to get more crowded with time.

'I hate tears baby. Come, I have something special for you,' Iona tells Adrika.

'Where are you guys going?' Arjun asks. His voice drowning in the noise. Ved calls Arjun backstage. It was freezing. Adrika wraps her arms around herself.

'What are you doing? I don't want to miss the dance. Let's go,' Arjun says.

'Wait…wait…wait,' Iona says. Iona shoves her hands into her pockets. All eyes are on her.

'What are you doing?' Adrika wants to know.

Iona taks out two bottles from each pocket.

'What's this?' Ved asks.

'V-O-D-K-A. I wanted to make this fest, our last one together, special.'

'What if anyone sees us?' says Arjun looking around. He moves closer to the wall in the darkness.

'They will throw us out of college, but I have all reasons to take this risk,' Iona winks at Adrika.

'Yeah, yeah,' Ved puts one hand on Arjun's shoulder and another on Adrika's shoulder. They stand in a small circle now, just like Ved did before the match.

They hold each other's hand saying, 'No matter how old we become, we are friends forever.

'Forever.'

'Forever.'

'Forever.' They clink their bottles.

Adrika thinks about her departure from college in a few months. Everyone will be enjoying the last few months together. Time is ditching her.

Should she be happy or sad?

The things she read in the books, she now realizes—you can't have everything.

She looks confused. A few tears fall from her eyes but some collapse on the shoulders of her friends, some on their hands and some between her smiling lips.

Eight

A Few months later

ADRIKA HAS MIXED feelings about joining office in Mumbai. It is a major step for her, she has to leave her family and become more independent. Though she has lived in a hostel, things are going to be different for her without her friends. Happiness is visible on her mother's face. She has seen Adrika go through the various colours of life. Moreover, they both have achieved a significant success.

Adrika misses Arjun the most among all her friends during her initial phase of training. Probably because they are both homesick. Her mother has been there with her during her training period.

Now, it was time to leave home. Forever. Now, she will only come home during festivals or when time permits. Lucknow will be just in her memories now.

Adrika has ended her long vacation and now is the time to start a new life in a new city.

The sun is pouring in through the gaps in the curtains. It is a cold Sunday morning as she lies awake in bed, curled up within the confines of her blanket. The birds are chattering and the morning has begun with its many activities, yet everything seems gloomy to her.

At times, she calls up Iona to discuss this feeling with her, but considering Iona's happy-go-lucky life, she keeps her phone aside pressing the back button to skip calling her. Anyway, she knows that Iona will ask for some time and things will be fine one day. Life changes after college. A lot.

She wonders what is wrong with her life. At the moment, she feels things are getting better. She has a good job. She will repay all her education loan and will fix everything to have a good life. Her relatives have started questioning her mother about her marriage. Like relatives always do. She definitely wants to take her mother to Mumbai after the training gets over. Probably, she is afraid to leave her home.

It is not just her departure, which is making her weak. It's just that her dreams have never come true. Therefore, she does not want to think anything good. She is scared of losing it. We all have a dark past that we are not particularly proud of. Whenever she is alone, she starts thinking about her past and that makes her uneasy. There are so many memories, ones that made her happy. Yet the overwhelming memories are the ones allied with negative emotions. She thinks of her past, the frustrations which seem to have gripped her life. However, she has managed well, but it's been so difficult to fake in front of those friends who never hide anything from her.

She tries to be stronger emotionally. But whenever she runs away from her past and memories, they seem to follow her, haunt her.

Maybe, these thoughts are running in her mind because she is going away from her friends and family. Failing in first love does not mean she will fail again. She agrees, but what if she goes through the same situation again. That thought makes it scarier. She has to come out of it. Perhaps her busy schedule and a little more time will heal everything in a new city.

She never told Iona that that day when she asked about the

bottles and packets of cigarette in her room. She was the one who was consuming this to get rid of her pain that she has gone through. She rarely drinks but that day when nobody was there to share her happiness, she felt completely alone. A bottle of vodka could not make anything right but loneliness took over her senses, and she could not control herself. Eventually, she slept off in her balcony and woke up cold and shivering.

Adrika is about to say something but looking at her mother, she skips the idea of discussing things with her.

♥

'And don't travel in local buses if you don't feel comfortable, Adrika!' Her mother gets continuously worried.

All mothers are same for their kids, irrespective of gender. Her mother reminds her of everything that she thinks Adrika will forget. Adrika is not used to travelling in buses, not even Volvo buses. If ever she does, she starts feeling restless. Her friends say that she is still immature. However, it does not look so, neither physically nor mentally. She is the highest paid, gorgeous, intelligent chocolate taster among her friends now.

'You have been repeating these things for the last four years,' Adrika replies, rolling on her bed and checking her phone.

'Yes, because you haven't changed from college days,' retorts her mother. Adrika looks at her and smiles.

'Many things have changed.'

No one speaks.

Many of the times, time teaches us things that we are afraid to do ever in life.

'Adrika! Get up, you have your flight.'

'Adrika, check your bag if everything is there or not. I have kept dry fruits and laddoo in the trolley bag. Eat them rather than just sharing with people.'

'I am new to that place, and I don't know anybody. I only have to eat them.' Her words express her spirits. Her mother is doing everything from early morning, things she has been doing for years. Taking care of everything.

'Adrika…'

Adrika walks in her room from the sofa where she has slept for an hour after getting up early in fear of leaving home. She picks her handbag, then throws it in the corner, and sits on the bed.

'Adrika, it's okay beta. You can come back whenever you want, and everyone has to leave home for work. And everyone was saying that I am so lucky that my daughter got not just the best but one of the highest paid jobs, isn't it?' her mother tries to pamper and help her homesickness that she has always gone through whenever she has to leave home. She does not understand much about her job, but others say her daughter has done well. That makes her happy and satisfied.

'Ma, I can go to the airport by myself. You stay here.'

'I haven't seen the airport. I'll come to drop you,' her mother replies. Adrika does not want her to come along. She will not be able to stop her tears. She will make her go weak and her mother just wants to drop her safely.

The first solo journey is always unique and memorable, but she forgets the other side of it. So, on mutual agreement that nobody will cry, they both reach Lucknow airport.

♥

Adrika can break into tears any moment so she chooses to smile instead and calmly waves goodbye to her mother while entering the airport. Her mother wants her to turn back but she does not. Turning back would make both weaker. She rushes to the check-in counter as she is already running late, but the flight is on time. She collects her boarding pass by breaking the queue, by requesting other passengers.

There are different kinds of people there. The smell of sweet perfume mingles with the smell of jet fuel. She recognizes the smell of fading perfumes that the women are wearing. That does not really help her to come out from her emotional trauma. The whir of wheels on marble and concrete mix with the mechanical, yet pleasant, voices on the public-address systems calling for someone to go to the nearest courtesy phone, or announcing that flight 6E 304 is now boarding at gate four, 'Passengers travelling to Mumbai kindly proceed to gate number four. Thank you!'

She walks towards gate number four after a fast track security check. Managing her handbag in one hand, boarding pass and cell phone in the other, she runs. She has a scarf around her neck along with earphones. Adrika steps into the flight and gets into her seat. The memorable boarding. She had asked for the window seat so that she could avoid the public display of her tears. She puts on her earphones and removes them. She opens a notebook and closes. She does not know what she really needs. So many things are going on in her head. She starts crying remembering her past, missing her mother, friends and out of fear of loneliness. She breaks into tears. Her mother never wanted her to go away but all the way she motivated and kept her excited for her arrival in the city of hearts. She has always encouraged her to move on in life and taught her to accept everything that comes on the way. Adrika remembers what she had said when she was going through a tough time, that life always shows you everything that you don't want to see. So learn from it.

She is sniffling while looking out of the window. When she realizes that someone is watching her, she wipes her tears and goes to the lavatory. She closes the door and cries uncontrollably, tears streaming down her face. She feels a vacuum in her stomach. She takes time and washes her face once she realizes that someone has knocked the door twice.

'Sorry,' says Adrika to the woman waiting outside and goes back to her seat. She takes out a book from her handbag and gets comfortable.

'Are you okay?' a person sitting at the aisle asks.

Adrika turns around, consciously hiding her face, 'Yeah, I am fine.' She smiles and turns the first page of the book she is holding, pretending to read. She does not want anyone to look at her.

One page is jumping on another, with silence and wet eyes, she sleeps holding that book in her hand before an air hostess comes and wakes her up.

Nine

A FOYER LEADING TO a sitting area furnished with a sofa, armchairs and tea table—Adrika looks happy entering one of the finest hotels. This feels like a vacation after a sponsored flight ticket and then a stay at a four-star hotel. Till yesterday, she was just taking it like any other job but now she is taking it seriously. She walks in to all the corners of the room. Pulling the curtain up, she picks up the check-in pamphlet from the table and enters the password to connect to WiFi. She walks towards the window and looks out.

She is definitely going to enjoy the stay. The room overlooks the courtyard and is decorated with rich fabrics, classical art and wooden furniture. Everything is meticulously decorated and the room features a cozy bed and sitting area with a desk. She tells herself that leaving home for this job is not a wrong decision. She wonders why her father never described these comforts of finding a job. Probably because he always insisted her to go for government jobs. She misses his presence and wishes she could call him once to say that she has grown up to fulfil his dreams.

She takes a bottle of water from the minibar. The minibar reminds her of her friends. She is missing that clink of bottles with her friends. Ved had said on the day of the fest, 'Friends forever.' She questions that promise.

Arjun and Ved are much more excited about their reunion in the same city after a few weeks when their college is over. They also have had pre-joining trainings in an IT firm as business analysts. Destiny is pulling everyone at the same place again. Perhaps.

♥

Exquisitely prepared bed linen, interiors bathed in warm light, and a smile on her face prove that life changes over time.

Adrika drags her giant trolley bag to the rack in the corner of the room.

Her phone flashes with a call.

'I have just reached the hotel, Mamma. Now, I really do not believe that I deserve this job. Yeah, it's a good hotel and I am going to stay here for around two weeks. Fifteen days to be precise,' Adrika has just started making plans to roam around in Mumbai. Her mother must be happy that she would not take any time to adjust herself to a new city. Moreover, these days she keeps messaging Arjun and Ved to keep an eye on her once they reach Mumbai. All mothers are the same.

Ding-dong. The doorbell rings.

'Ma! I will call you after sometime,' she disconnects the call.

She opens the door.

'Ma'am, are you comfortable? Please let me know if you need anything?'

'Yes, I am good. Thanks!'

Adrika sits on the sofa and messages Iona on WhatsApp and waits for her reply. She is definitely going to miss her in Mumbai. Mostly, when she has to go for shopping. Now she will realize it is not an easy task.

The things they have done together in college! Good. Bad. Worst. She messages Ved when she does not get a reply from Iona. She is curious to know whether Arjun and Ved are coming to Mumbai or going to Chennai. Arjun is a north Indian and cannot even think of living in Chennai. Probably life will teach him everything soon.

Hey, what's up my WhatsApp boy?

Hey, what's up?

I am good.

You tell, how is Mumbai treating you?

Adrika misses them. Everything has changed so fast.

It's nice as of now.

These people are treating me as if I am a princess.

Ved typing...

You are princess, isn't it?

Still if you don't think so wait for the end of the month when you will get the first salary.

Haha, let's see.

Well, I am missing you all.

I wish you all were here.

Are you guys coming to Mumbai or Chennai, any update?

It will take some time to adjust.

Why don't you check out guys in your batch until we come there.

LOL

Shut up.

Sometimes, rejection of suggestions welcome new thoughts. Adrika takes a pause to think. What is his take on life?

What shut up? It's high time now.

I don't want to see you dying single.

Adrika lays on the bed, laughing, and picks up the menu from the table. Then suddenly she realizes that her mother had packed food for her journey that she had forgotten to eat.

She asks him again. However, it seems Ved is disappointed or they have decided to give her surprise.

Are you guys coming to Mumbai?

Next week.

She jumps up from her bed in surprise. She cannot believe it as Ved teases her all the time. She has learnt one thing with him, don't get excited until it is on paper.

What? Are you kidding?

Just 6 more days.

Seriously?

I am not joking.

Yes, Arjun's wishes have worked out. LOL

That is nice.

She controls her happiness and decides to call Arjun, not for the further confirmation but to congratulate him.

Listen, I am hungry.

Let me eat something.

I will call you in the night.

Congratulations you both.

Lol, okay.

Enjoy your time. Bye!

Bye!

She looks happier now. Things are already falling in place for her. Only a few get lucky to meet old friends. She wishes Iona could also skip the idea of travelling the globe and come to Mumbai. Life would be much better.

She gets up, opens her bag, and skips the idea of ordering

from the menu. She has been a discus champion from her school days and it is easily visible from the way she throws the menu on the bed—just near the table where it was kept earlier.

She keeps the tiffin on the table. We all become kids when we connect to our memories. While taking things out of her trolley bag and handbag, she starts turning the pages of her diary that she has been carrying with her for years. She reads a page. She smiles and closes it.

While groping for things in her handbag, she finds a strange note, which says—

Hi, I really don't know what is your problem, which is making you helpless. I don't know it's acrophobia or homesickness or a heartbreak or something else which is making you cry. Don't cry. Everything takes time but things change in our favour and we smile again. I used to cry a lot when I was going through a tragic heartbreak and when I left my home for the first time—just like you. In the washroom. It's okay.

Keep smiling :)

Your co-passenger, who is still figuring out his life.

She tries to guess who might have kept this note in her handbag—the young man who was sitting next to her in the flight? Probably.

Holding the note in her hand, she touches the words with her thumb. She has only seen this in movies but in reality, there are still good people who care about others.

Or maybe he was just trying to hit on her, her mind says before her heart accepted the good side of it.

Whatever, he didn't hurt her in any way.

She easily connects this to her life.

She suddenly turns the note and tries to find the name of the author of the note. There is nothing else written on it. She goes through the words again to get a clue. Sometimes names are hidden in words. Her idea does not work out. He even asked her if everything was okay. She had smiled and rudely, paused the conversation. She regrets not asking his name. Few things are good to do for no reasons. She keeps the note safely in a secret pocket of her handbag where she only keeps a photo of her parents.

She enjoys the meal and takes a nap for a while imagining about the stranger in the flight. Sometimes we get happiness in unusual things but sometimes even our own memories give us pain.

She dozes off while messaging Iona about the note.

Ten

IT HAS BEEN more than three weeks since they first wanted to meet at one place. Today is Arjun's birthday. It is the time when everyone has to gather at his place else they will have to listen to his taunts till his next birthday. Precaution is always better than cure. Except Ved, nobody needs a reminder of his birthday.

Half of the day has gone in sleeping as the party already started the previous night. Arjun, Ved and a few of their mutual friends had come over. They had partied hard until they were tired and slept wherever they got a place in the hall and rooms, and one was found in the lobby near the kitchen. One by one, everyone left. Ved could only hear footsteps when somebody tiptoed out of the hall.

A cold chill runs through Ved's calves as he is still sleeping and alarm is ringing along with beeps of a drained battery.

Ved manages to get up and take a walk through the messy room. It's 2.30 p.m. He finds no one around except a few empty bottles, pieces of cake, candles, chips and candy wrappers, which are swirling in the corner with the wind.

He has a bad hangover; he is dizzy, has a headache and feels feverish. Last night, Arjun had asked him not to drink too much but he was late in convincing him. It's difficult to stop him when it's a house party and he is already drunk—no fear, just wine and beer! He sits on a chair and drinks water from a bottle. He tries to recall the things he did last night. He really does not want to remember because the last thing he remembers is that he had danced madly with Arjun. He takes a few more sips of water and checks WhatsApp. He walks up to Arjun's room to check when Adrika would be coming. There is no one in the room. He takes out his phone to call Arjun, but his phone is not reachable. He drops a WhatsApp messages to Arjun.

Where are you?

He waits for few minutes for a reply but nothing happens. Just as he begins scrolling through his contact list, the doorbell rings and Ved rushes to open the door. Though he is good at making guesses, but this was unusual.

'Where have you been dude?' Ved asks.

'Nowhere, I went to the gurudwara for service,' says Arjun.

There is always something different on his birthday. This year, Arjun had decided to go for a service in a gurudwara. Even if he is not too religious, going to a service in an unfamiliar religion can be enlightening and a great way to meet new people. Arjun loves that. It gives him profound happiness.

Every friend has a habit that you don't like. Ved is talkative when Arjun wants to be quiet. He does not like to take Ved along with him. He enjoys his own time. Unaccompanied.

♥

Nothing could be worse than your best friend not having anything planned for your birthday. Arjun tries hard to know if there is any plan. He does not want to spend the time sitting at home, at least not on his birthday. Well, Arjun deserves to know nothing today. He has always been late to wish others on their birthdays—as you sow, so you reap.

Adrika and Anushka must have something in their minds,

as they had not wished him yet.

Arjun cannot force anyone to wish him and say, 'Wish me, it's my birthday.' However, at least he expected his best friends to give him surprises. At least a message over WhatsApp.

It's four in the evening and Ved has looked at his watch a number of times. Ved has managed everything so well and pretended that today is just like any other day. He has definitely learnt to give surprises. Today is the day to show his creativity.

The doorbell rings while Arjun is sitting on the sofa, scrolling through his Facebook page. It feels irritating sometimes. Dimpy Aunty was right when she said that he has become addicted to gadgets and obsessed about social media. Maybe he has achieved them by working hard. Whatever, sometimes he crosses the limit when Ved finds him taking calls from the washroom. Arjun, on the other hand, believes it saves time.

Really? It is the height of obsession! Well, ignore him. He is peculiar at times.

Ved makes a paper ball and throws it hard at him. That breaks his attention.

'Arjun open the door,' Ved says leaning back on the sofa.

'Please open it, you are sitting closer to it,' Arjun applies Pythagoras theorem and convinces Ved that he has no option to say no.

Busy with his cell phone Arjun has forgotten that every day is not his birthday, and from tomorrow he has to live a normal life and pay for his deeds.

Ved gets up and snatches his cell phone away.

'What did I do?' he asks. His frustration at having no plans for his birthday is quite visible in his expressions.

'Get up and open the door,' Ved purposely wants him to open the door. Probably that is the part of the plan, if Ved has any.

Arjun reaches the door with lazy steps and looks through the peephole.

'You are not surrounded by criminals. Open the door,' teases Ved.

♥

Adrika is standing outside. As soon as Arjun opens the door, she wishes him loudly and gives him a long warm hug at the door. A long tight hug is more precious than a gift. It stays forever.

Nothing changes when they meet. The annoyed face turns into a big smile. Adrika pushes a shoe in between the door and frame. Probably just to keep the door open. Ved notices it.

She enters the room happily waving at Ved.

Adrika is wearing a dress that makes her look even cuter and perfectly complements her slim waist and toned upper body. Dressing up rarely matters to her because whatever she wears looks good on her. Her colleagues say that she is supposed to look mature not cute at this age. Enjoying her transition from teenage to maturity, Adrika is living a happy life.

More footsteps are heard outside and Anushka appears at the door. She follows them straight to the hall.

'I knew it,' Arjun says and welcomes Anushka. They rarely hug each other. Probably they do behind the walls. Who knows?

Anushka is looking gorgeous in a pinstripe skirt and jacket over a dark purple blouse. She is wearing her only pair of designer heels that she wears occasionally.

'Sometimes you look like my favourite old movie,' says Arjun when only she could hear him.

'Probably old wine is the right word,' Anushka winks. She enjoys pulling his leg. Actually, everyone enjoys pulling his leg.

She sits next to Ved on the sofa.

'Hey! Today is his birthday and you are lying like a lazy bum. What's wrong with you?' Anushka gives Ved a light punch on his ribs. They have become decent friends over the months.

'Looking good,' Ved appreciates Adrika and Anushka. Anushka nods with a smile.

'You have also changed a lot,' Adrika says to Arjun sitting on the sofa. Ved pops up in between, 'I wish he could be like this in college days. He would have at least have had a pretty girl around.'

'Times change,' Anushka winks at him. They all laugh in sarcasm.

'Yes, I think so. Time changes,' Arjun larks and continues, 'I had no idea that I used to wear sports shoes with pants with old-fashioned grandfather glasses on my lean body with a clean shaven face. Let's not remember that. That's the only thing about college days I do not want to remember.'

'Chill! Everyone is like that in college days,' Anushka tells him.

'Leave this poor guy,' Adrika gives Arjun a jumbo box of chocolates and hands over the cake to Anushka.

Meeting old friends feels like reliving the days again. That's what Ved had said in his speech at the last fest at college. No matter how old we become, we are friends forever.

Forever.

Forever.

Forever.

♥

Adrika desperately wanted to meet them from the day she had come to Mumbai a week ago. Ved picks a few chocolates from the box and says, 'What's for me?'

'Hmm...well, it's not your birthday,' Adrika teases him by throwing some at him, 'I have special ones, for you.'

Her eyes glint as she looks at him.

'Why don't you start making chocolates?' Ved questions, unwrapping one of them and starts chewing.

'Probably some day,' she answers casually. Everyone has dreams to start something creative. Adrika has not discussed her dreams with anyone though.

'I'll wait for that day,' Ved nods. Arjun and Ved are very proud of Adrika—from where she had started her life and now... she has set a bar. Success is not where you reach, it is actually the journey of growing up with time.

'Let's cut the cake,' Anushka takes the cake out of the box and puts it at the centre of the table.

Ved swipes his finger at the corner of the box and licks the cream. Anushka pats on his hand. 'Don't do that.'

The cake looks tempting with a few cherries on it. Adrika lights two candles and sets them on the cake, but Arjun pulls out one of them, goes into his room to keep it in front of the idol of Lord Ganesh beside the photographs of his parents. Nobody has seen it yet, else others may tease him. Anushka follows him too.

Three continuous rings happen at the door.

♥

They must have planned a surprise for me, Arjun guesses. However, he is not expecting much. The amazing cake and candles have taken most of his attention.

Adrika keeps looking at her handbag and the stranger's note that is sticking out of it. Some complex algorithm runs in her mind. She gets up to open the door and pushes the note inside the bag.

A tall, attractive man with short hair appears. It is Sumrit.

The one who had won the football match at the college fest. Sumrit smells of fresh soap and an old intense perfume. Moreover, he looks like a corporate person wearing a shirt with jeans, holding a bouquet in one hand and a phone in the other. That's life for him these days.

Sumrit is currently doing an MBA from Welingkar Institute.

'Hey,' Ved greets him, 'how are you?'

'I am good,' Sumrit replies cheerfully with a broad smile. He steps inside.

'I am sorry guys. I got late,' he apologizes. Arjun walks up and welcomes him with a hug.

'Hey mate, wish you a very happy birthday,' Sumrit says.

'You have arrived at the right time,' Arjun makes him comfortable. He knew that Sumrit was in the city but could not get an opportunity to catch up with him.

Though Ved and Sumrit were playing against each other in college days, they had always been good friends off the ground. Their bond has become stronger because at times Sumrit accompanied Ved to practices even when he was not planning to make this into a career.

When Adrika mentioned Sumrit while Ved was planning things for today, he invited him as well.

Sumrit is not talkative but enjoys humour. He is deep and intense with his thoughts. If they meet more often, then it will not take much time to make their bond stronger so that they can call him up for weekend nights out.

'Hi,' Adrika looks at Sumrit and smiles.

Before Anushka feels left out in the conversation, Ved introduces Anushka to Sumrit. They must have seen each other in college but they had never met or hung out together.

First impression stays forever; Anushka knows it well. They

both greet each other. Sometimes sophistication is a good start to a sensible conversation.

♥

Holding a knife in his hand, waiting for everyone to settle down, Arjun stands in front of the cake wearing the birthday hat.

'There you go…' they say in unison, as they begin singing the birthday song for Arjun.

Arjun takes a long gulp of air and blows the candle as if he had practised before. He cut the cake delicately.

Who gets the first bite?

It does not matter among them.

Probably it does now. He takes a piece and turns towards Anushka, who is standing next to Adrika. Has he chosen her intentionally? Before they could speak or react, Sumrit smears a big piece of cake on Arjun's face. Arjun's neck and shoulders are now covered in cake. Adrika winks and takes the bottle from Ved and pours water over Arjun. That is what she has been waiting for so long. After college, the practice of emptying a bucket over someone's head has now reduced to using a bottle; the crowd had reduced to just a few heads, but their bond got stronger with these moments, which stays on forever no matter how old they grow. They want to cherish and make it unforgettable, as they always did.

'I am shivering,' Arjun says while ducking and turning his other cheek every time they put more cake on his face.

'You should not forget your first birthday in Mumbai for the rest of your life,' says Adrika in jest, playing with his hair.

'I won't. I won't.' Arjun begs her to stop. The weather is not that cold outside but ice water really does feel cold in the middle of the night.

'I will just come back,' he could only say that. Everyone enjoys the cake and settles down on the sofa. Sumrit pours juice in glasses, and passes one to Adrika.

'It's juice, right?' she asks peeping into the glass.

'Yes, just juice.'

He adds, 'I saw you clinking the glass backstage.'

Adrika takes time to respond, 'Backstage?' She recalls the last fest night in college that they had spent together.

'You saw us,' she laughs aloud.

Adrika tells Anushka what had happened that day, still laughing.

Ved puts on some music. That adds to the celebrations.

'You are getting medicines for me if I fall ill,' Arjun appears in the hall with a hairdryer.

'For that, you have to fall ill first,' Adrika is getting her pace back. She is enjoying after a very long time.

♥

Ved brings in a big watermelon with a few straws. Adrika helps Sumrit to take the hookah out of Ved's room and places it in the centre of the hall. Anushka gets chips and potato swirls from the kitchen.

'This is for all of you,' Ved says, being the host of this reunion.

Sumrit lights the hookah.

'Don't worry, it is flavoured hookah. It doesn't taste like tobacco at all,' Ved tells Adrika.

'Okay, okay,' she says.

Arjun starts connecting the dots and figures out what Ved has been doing from the morning. There must be something thrilling. Ved usually liked to do crazy stuff.

'What's this?' Adrika asks curiously, pointing at the watermelon.

'Drunken watermelon,' he says instantly in excitement as if he is ready to speak even before Adrika can ask. Everyone looks at him. The name itself defines that it is going to be a boozy night. Ved grins and keeps the watermelon in a position so it does not roll over. It seems Ved has drilled a big hole in the centre. Ved has done some crazy things. Experience always helps us understand things better. Anushka observes things around her.

'Oh wow, natural watermelon shake,' Adrika relishes these kinds of creative things. Probably that is the reason she has one of the most creative jobs. Ved's efforts have attracted everyone.

'It's not just a watermelon shake,' Ved snorts.

'Vodka watermelon?' Adrika looks at him.

'Yes.'

'I knew it the moment you appeared. How can I not know you?'

Ved suddenly adds, 'Wait. I made one more thing.' He runs to the kitchen and comes back with a plate of scooped strawberries standing upright like on a chessboard.

'Ved is now presenting to you the most sensational birthday special, Strawberry Shots,' Ved sets the plate on the table next to the watermelon. The excitement has reached the next level. The strawberries are shining with icy drops on the top.

'When did you do all this?' Anushka asks.

Ved looks at Arjun and says, 'When he was sleeping.'

Being in a relationship actually changes a person. The laziest bum in college days has become the most creative mind. Relationship changes the person. Yes. It does.

Adrika says, showing her displeasure at the sight of vodka watermelon, 'You guys carry on.'

'It is just vodka with watermelon shake, you can have it.

It's your best friend's birthday, take this,' Ved offers her a straw.

She looks at Arjun, who says, 'Nothing wrong with a few sips. Enjoy the time. I'll drop you.'

Arjun remembers very well how soon it starts affecting her senses. She nods.

'Cheers to Arjun!' Ved shouts, all raising their straws.

'Cheers!'

'Cheers!'

'Cheers!'

♥

The music becomes louder, and the air inside becomes hazier. The smoke in the hall is swirling around. As time passes, a few rounds of drinks and strawberry shots drag them from the sofa to floor. They sit comfortably. They agree that house parties are much better than nights out. Holding the pipe in her hand and taking a long puff from it, Adrika smiles looking at everyone and nods, saying, 'Now may we all request Arjun to play the guitar for us.' She passes the pipe to Sumrit, the coal on top burns violently as he sucks it in.

'Yay! He should do something,' a drunk Ved says.

'What do you mean by he should do something?' Arjun asks.

Anushka laughs and clarifies shaking the ice cubes in her glass, 'He means that we are entertaining you for hours. Now it's your turn.'

Arjun knows what they are asking for, he pretends to cough a little.

'Don't pretend that you have a cold,' Adrika catches him the next moment.

'I am taking you guys shopping tomorrow, what else do

you need?' Arjun replies hoping his words would be taken into consideration.

'So what? That's a tradition you have to follow,' Anushka says. Ved and Adrika agree. Yes, tradition. It's not about buying many things but Arjun takes them for shopping every year on his birthday. Once he had said that birthdays are just to spread happiness. They took it seriously.

Ved gets his guitar and gives him to start with the song that he croons in the washroom.

'This is what we are talking about.' Sumrit speaks out. He never knew about Arjun's hidden talent. Well, he has many hidden talents that only Dimpy Aunty knows about.

Arjun picks the guitar and his fingers fall in the frets. They follow him without knowing the rhythm. The smoke twists forming curls in the gloom, illuminated only by the age-speckled purple light in the hall. The jokes get funnier; Arjun becomes a comedian of epic proportions. They party hard until they are bushed.

♥

It is not just in the morning when all clocks run faster. It also runs faster when you are having a good time with your loved ones. It is 12.30 a.m. when Adrika notices a message on WhatsApp.

'Guys! I should leave now. Tomorrow, I have to get up early.' Adrika announces as if nobody is listening to her.

'Wait I'll drop you both,' Arjun says looking at Anushka and Adrika. Arjun was like that ideal father who becomes a kid with kids but makes sure at the end of the day that they all reach home safely. Moreover, Adrika is new to the city and he has become more protective of her over time.

'No, I can go. It's just 12.30,' Adrika says while Arjun appears to be wearing a jacket and putting on his shoes.

'Are you sure?' Anushka asks Arjun.

'I am not going to drive. We'll get a cab,' he replies.

'I am also leaving, so I'll drop you on the way,' Sumrit says. Arjun pauses and looks at Adrika if she is comfortable to go with him.

'Are you sure?' Arjun asks her. He expects to hear a no.

'Yes we can go,' Adrika says, 'I think we are on the same route,' she looks at Sumrit, who nods in agreement.

'Are you sure?' the same way Anushka had asked Arjun a minute before.

'Yes, I am fine. You have fun and take care of him,' she replies and points towards Ved who was drunk.

'Shut up, I am fine,' Ved replies.

'That we can see.'

'Okay then, thanks for coming and making my birthday so special.'

Adrika takes a step ahead and gives him a tight hug, 'You deserve more than this. God bless you.' She waves to Ved.

'Enjoy buddy,' Sumrit says and leaves.

'Hey Adrika, you forgot this,' Anushka hands over a piece of paper.

'Oh! Thanks,' she takes it and puts it into her handbag.

Eleven

THEY REACH ADRIKA'S place by 1.30 a.m. She realizes that it is too late for her neighbours.

'Shall I drop you upstairs?' Sumrit asks her as she looks a little tired and shaky, though she is not drunk. Perhaps her high heels would make it difficult for her to take the stairs. Why do girls wear heels when they already have a good height? Maybe, something extra is always better. Nowadays, when the whole world is transforming and talking about women empowerment, Sumrit feels it is okay to walk with a taller girl.

'No, I am perfectly fine. Thanks for dropping me,' her hands grip his, her eyes roll back and she senses a headache.

'Come, you need me,' Sumrit walks her upstairs. He comes to know about the reality before she pretends anymore.

'Maybe I do.' Adrika removes her heels and tiptoes to the stairs that take her to the second floor.

Sumrit follows her.

'Am I too drunk?' she asks him in confusion.

'Sleep and take rest,' Sumrit replies. Even he is not very sure of himself.

Adrika unlocks the door. She does not want her neighbours to know about her arrival at this time.

'Not sure if you should come inside as many of my colleagues are my neighbours,' Adrika says looking around and finds her next-door-neighbour closing the door. She takes a step back behind the wall.

'I can't come here? I am not a stranger,' Sumrit replies, taking the keys from her and opening the door.

'Not like that. Of course, you are not a stranger. Okay come inside,' Adrika calls him in.

'I'll leave in some time. Don't worry, nobody has seen us entering,' Sumrit enters and Adrika follows him.

The door shuts with a gust of wind.

Sumrit sits on the sofa in the hall. She tilts her head towards the edge of the sofa. She does not seem to be in her senses.

'Let's go to the room and switch off the lights here. This is directly visible from there,' she points towards a giant sliding window, which could be easily viewable from the other side of the apartment. Others may see what's happening inside.

'No wait,' she pulls the curtains rather than going into her room. She does not want anything to happen, as both of them are drunk.

'It is fine,' she smiles and just to sidetrack the conversation she asks, 'You need water?'

'No, I'm good. You look dizzy and sleepy.'

He looks at her with amusement. Her hair is a mess and her cheeks are flushed red as if she has fever. She feels feverish when she drinks on an empty stomach. When Iona was with her, she used to fill half of her stomach with food and the rest with alcohol. A strip of her bra is exposed on her shoulder and she seems to be losing her control and senses too.

♥

Adrika and Sumrit have been dating since the last day of college fest. Six months to be precise. It all began with the message she had ignored. Before that, she took time to convince herself. They had a secret plan to come to Mumbai that nobody knew of.

Not even her best friends. Love does not come with guarantee, it is like a game of bluff; if you find the right person, it works out for life and if you do not, you cannot blame yourself for that.

Adrika has taken time to get into a relationship but she has engaged herself with faith, trust and belief. She has found a best friend like Ved in Sumrit unlike her previous relationship.

When he cares, he cares like a mother and listens like a father when she needs him most. When she shares her secrets, she shares like his sister, when she cries he is always there to pamper her. Sumrit makes her feel special like no one has ever done before.

She is trying to find the courage to tell Arjun and then Iona, who have always wanted her to get into a relationship. A relationship makes things more beautiful. A relationship becomes the solution for all problems, but sometimes a cause too. However, Adrika is ready to make this relationship smoother and happier as she has always dreamt of.

A good relationship turns a house into a home. It makes you a responsible and mature person.

♥

They are standing at the centre of the hall. They can see each other's faces and she feels the touch of Sumrit's fingers on the tip of her fingers.

'I'll help you sleep,' he comes a step closer. He taps on her feet to get her attention. She may not be able to balance herself. 'What are you doing?' she says suddenly and hangs on his shoulder.

'Don't do anything with me. I warn you,' she laughs. She is staggering. He touches her lips and moves three fingers around giving rest to his thumb and baby finger. Maybe he would use them later in his acts of love.

'I am not going to drink again,' she giggles and jabs at his stomach. She swings in that moment.

'I am always there to hold you, isn't it?' He feels the warmth of her breath on his lips. There is no hesitation between them. He also did not want to let the moment go away. Therefore, he rectifies the situation by claiming an intense kiss as if she has been waiting for it. He moves his fingers around her back, which makes her heart beat faster.

Fearing that if she blinks, the moment would end, she holds him tightly as she feels like sharing many things with him. Perhaps once they diffuse the fire within, she can. Things were moving smoothly. Wanting her to give an approval to go ahead and explore her body, he holds her tightly in his arms, tighter; so does she. She has expressed no intention to leave him now. Instead, she enjoys his breath around her neck.

♥

Sumrit gets up realizing that half of the night has passed. He pulls his shirt from the corner and buttons up his jeans. Adrika drags a t-shirt from the chair placed near the sofa and puts it on.

She takes a few sips of water. Perhaps she will finish some of her work before she signs off for bed.

'It's late. You can stay here and leave early morning. But you have to get up before seven,' she does not want him to travel late at night unaccompanied as he is drunk. In fact, she does not want to be alone like this. She wants to talk, she wants to share things at this moment. Girls do have their timings to share and experience things.

'Then I am perfectly fine to go home,' says Sumrit.

Pronunciation of words define the attention you are giving to someone. However, Sumrit hasn't understood what Adrika really means with her words, that she wants to be with him.

'Okay,' she leers standing right in front of him. Undoubtedly, a hug would be the end of their conversation before he leaves.

She does an audit of the hall and helps him find his stuff. Some were behind the sofa, some were under it.

In the deep silence of midnight, they hug under the roof and Sumrit leaves.

Door closes.

Going back to her room, she looks in the mirror. She pushes her collar behind the curls and touches her mole. She moves to another one on her neckline. She feels how she has felt him. She smiles and pinches the mole on her décolletage harshly exactly the way he has done a few moments ago.

She realizes that she has to post a letter to one of her friends on her birthday tomorrow. She believes that no matter where technology reaches, nothing can replace the feelings of letter writing and reading. Writing a letter makes a bond stronger that you just cannot break by deleting them on Facebook. It is a magical feeling to read or write one.

She goes to the hall to retrieve her handbag. She finds the stranger's note torn into pieces on the corner of the table. Adrika and Sumrit had an argument when she had showed it to him. She pauses and takes those pieces and throws them into the dustbin. She does not want to do anything that may hurt Sumrit or this budding relationship. Every relationship has its ups and downs and she is definitely going to manage things well. As of now, she is just thinking of finding a way to tell Arjun and others about her relationship.

Twelve

It's Sunday morning after the night before. She gets up at 5.30 a.m. and completes her assignment and sleeps for some time, and as usual, time runs on the horse.

She also calls to check whether Ved has done it or not. Otherwise, she'll have to sit with him in the breakout area during class. Adrika and Ved have joined French classes to learn a new language.

Moreover, she just cannot put into words the way she is feeling right now. She feels like calling Iona and talking to her. She ends up simply checking her cell phone.

The taste in her mouth, the splitting headache. She carefully levers up an eyelid and quickly shuts it back. A merciless sunbeam squirts straight into her eyes, making her head ache.

The lovely previous night… Effects of clinks, hangover of the fun she had with Arjun, Ved, Anushka and Sumrit. That has changed her last night. Losing herself in the battle of thoughts, she is trying to find ways to tell Arjun about Sumrit, that she is happier now and that she can spend her life with him.

Her phone rings as she is still tossing around on the bed. Adrika swipes her thumb indolently.

'Hello,' she answers sluggishly and leisurely leaves her grip on the bed. She finally breaks all relationships with her bed. Chucking the blanket to the other side, she snatches her towel as if she is a gymnast.

♥

'You told me to wake you up and I have been calling you for the last thirty minutes and you are not picking up my calls. Either you get up or you do not dare to tell me to wake you up again. I am not going to pick you up now.' Ved sounds irritated and enraged. He must be. He has not even called Iona so many times. She would have picked just after ten or fifteen times. However, consciously or subconsciously, being ignored is not acceptable to him.

'Sorry I was taking a bath and took a nap as you were running late.' Girls are never wrong in their own eyes.

'I am standing outside your apartment and calling.'

'Don't behave like a girlfriend. What's the time?' she asks. She is probably holding her cell phone between her shoulder and ear, and eating cornflakes at the same time.

'Eight-forty-five,' he speaks the digits clearly to make her realize how much time she has already wasted. He continues, 'Now don't eat, and come soon. We'll get late.'

'You should definitely not skip breakfast. I know you and your lazy roommate do not eat on time. I am getting something for you. Just give me five more minutes.'

'I am counting…' Ved says and disconnects the call.

It is a myth that over a period of time, we stop missing people. In fact, we miss them more. We just try to find a replacement so that either we do not get time to recall old memories or we meet new people to overwrite them. We are humans and genuinely we never forget. We just pretend.

Adrika has spent a good time in the last couple of weeks in Mumbai. As she has also joined French classes to learn a foreign language. Hopefully, after getting the certification, she will have more opportunities. This is how she wants to spend her free time—in a more productive manner. Moreover, if everything works out fine, Ved may even get a chance to be a part of the

Belgian football team by the end of the year. Being with Arjun he has learnt to take whatever comes your way, irrespective of whether it gives instant results or not. Therefore, he has also joined the same batch as Adrika.

♥

Beauty is not just about putting extra lip gloss or mascara; it is also about wearing anything but looking confident and carrying yourself with pride. Adrika looks adorable in a pair of jeans and shirt, taking long steps to go downstairs.

'Hey late bloomer,' Ved shouts from the other side of the road. Adrika turns around and finds Ved waving from a rickshaw. She crosses the road. The whole scene reminds them of their college days.

'Sorry for being late,' says Adrika.

'It's okay; I consider this as you being on time. I got late because of Arjun. He woke me up at six and then when I actually had to get up, I dozed off.'

She laughs aloud. The rickshaw driver looks at them in the side mirror.

'I have to leave early today from class. Dimpy Aunty is coming home,' says Ved.

'Dimpy Aunty…?' she takes time and asks.

'Dimpy Aunty…Anushka's mom. You met Anushka at the birthday party,' Ved reminds her.

'Yes, Arjun has told me a lot about her.'

'About Dimpy Aunty or Anushka?' Ved asks.

'Actually…both,' she replies and adds, 'Dimpy Aunty is quite funny, isn't she?'

'Quite is probably not the right word for her,' he grins.

'Well, Aunty wants to come to meet us. So I have to go

early today.'

'Cool, I can manage,' Adrika responds.

'Why don't you come with me?' asks Ved, who always has a plan for everything.

'No, you guys enjoy. I will come some other day. I have a few things to wrap up,' that last line implies that Adrika does not want to go. In fact, she does not want to miss her classes and that too during the initial few days. She hasn't changed till now. She is still the last person to take leave from office or bunk classes.

'You don't want to miss the class, right?' Ved knows her very well from college days. She looks at him and smiles.

'What else do you need in life?' Ved says in sarcasm.

'Chill! I'll come.'

The rickshaw stops and Ved pays him.

'Ved, come quickly, we're late already,' Adrika calls him from the other side of the road while he is busy counting the change that the rickshaw driver has given him.

'Now, what are you doing?' Adrika shows her cynicism at the way he is counting the coins.

'Coming, coming.'

It gives Adrika immense pleasure to learn new things. Learning a new language is one of those things because nobody judges you for your mistakes as all are learners. The fact is, the more educated we are, the more differences we create amongst us.

Ved and Adrika rush to the college entrance.

Walking through the lobby to reach their classroom, Adrika says, 'I have the worst record when it comes to reaching class on time.'

'Still, you have managed to score decently, more than Arjun and I ever have by waiting for you in every class you never reached on time,' Ved says looking at her while still walking.

Adrika does not speak, instead she blinks and flashes a broad smile.

'Chill, it's not like our college classes and frustrated professors. People here seem chilled out,' says Ved. He looks like he is convincing himself rather than assuring her. They are already late.

♥

'What are your names?' the person at the entry point asks with a big sardonic smile.

Adrika looks at Ved.

'What?' Ved asks.

'Nothing, I told you but you were busy collecting coins. Coins you saved, but nobody will save us now. Get ready to do some stupid things,' Adrika knows that now they have to do something. She is definitely not going to sing a song. While, she is more worried about Ved than about herself, she's wondering what joke he is going to crack to escape punishment for being late to class.

'He looks sweet, doesn't he?' he murmurs. Everyone else looks sweet except the people who teach engineering subjects.

'Wait,' says the man standing behind the podium. They both smile while looking at him.

'You are late, my friends, aren't you?' he asks the rest of the students sitting in the class.

'Yesss!' They both give a long approval.

'Sorry, Sir' they say in the same tone. Calm and soft.

'No, no that's okay. Don't be sorry. This is going to happen with everyone, anyway—some student or the other. Don't be sorry,' he smiles. The class sniggers at the scene.

They enter.

'Come here,' he calls them to the podium and continues, 'So what are your hobbies?'

Adrika answers, 'Sir, writing.'

'And yours?' he looks at Ved, who is busy thinking of an answer. When Ved does not respond, Adrika replies on his behalf, 'Sir, we are college friends. I know he is good at analyzing people.'

'What?' he hums.

She does not just want to save herself but Ved too. She is rectifying the situation.

'You write…would you like to share something with us?' he moves a step back and offers her the centre of the podium.

'Sure, Sir, but I need to think first. I'll sit there and write,' Adrika points towards the first row, which has a few seats empty because the rest of the class is sitting as far as possible from the podium.

He smiles and lets her take a seat.

'You also go,' he tells Ved. He has probably seen the expression on Ved's face.

'Thanks, Sir,' Ved sits next to Adrika, while cursing under his breath because she has chosen to sit in the first row. His cell phone vibrates in his pocket.

He somehow manages to check his phone. There is a message from Arjun saying that Aunty is reaching home in an hour and he needs him back as soon as possible.

Thirteen

NOT JUST INDIAN girls, but Indian boys also get conscious of certain things—marriage is one of those. Undoubtedly, Arjun should be the leader of those poor people. Dimpy Aunty has asked Ved if there is anything going on between Arjun and Anushka. Moreover, whenever Ved asks Arjun, he always changes the topic saying that they are just good friends.

However, Arjun is not sure about the purpose of Dimpy Aunty's visit, but there is definitely some reason behind it. He should not leave a single stone unturned.

Does she want to see how Arjun lives?

Does she think of any possibility of Arjun and Anushka getting married in the future? On the other hand, has his mother asked Dimpy Aunty to give him a surprise visit?

Then Arjun realizes that he has told neither Anushka nor Dimpy Aunty that he likes Anushka. How would they come to know? Ved has told him several times that he and Anushka are perfect for each other. Arjun always left the conversation midway, saying that he needs more time.

He says that love marriage has always been a tough effort in his Brahmin family where everyone had an arranged marriage, and the few who had the courage for love marriages were mistreated by the relatives. Therefore, it is not going to be an easy task for Arjun to convince his family even if he likes Anushka and sees a future with her. He should not forget that he has to sway his guarded mother, who is of the opinion that she will find him a good girl, towards the fact that Anushka is the right girl for him. What 'good' means in her dictionary, only God knows.

He ignores the stressful ideas and concentrates on his present; that makes more sense to him.

♥

Room? Check.

Fridge? Check.

Washroom? Check.

Dining table? Check.

Kitchen? Check.

Arjun goes through the checklist in his mind and realizes that Dimpy Aunty is even one step ahead of his mother. She reaches for places where even the cockroaches cannot. You cannot predict her moves. He revises.

Cupboard? Check.

Under the mattresses? Check.

WhatsApp Messages? Deleted.

Laptop? Umm, ignore.

WhatsApp group names? Changed.

All done. The house looks much cleaner than it was till a few hours ago. A lot actually.

Sometimes, the company you keep also matters when it comes to your life. Dimpy Aunty knows about Ved. Therefore, Arjun makes sure there is zero visibility of any kind of bottles, matchsticks and lighters in the house. He rechecks—there are no women's slippers, sandals or undergarments under the sofa.

He makes sure that the only things on the table are small write-ups, a notebook and a pen, and he thinks of replacing the ashtray with a flowerpot. That is all Arjun has to do to divert her mind from discussing irrelevant stuff. Dimpy Aunty loves his writing and the thoughts he puts on paper. He just needs to cash in on that today.

♥

Ved and Adrika leave the class early. Adrika messages Sumrit telling him that she is going to her friend's place. She does not mention the name of the friend. Mentioning the name means she is returning late at night, which Sumrit does not like.

Does that really matter? Probably it does for him. However, she avoids doing so. That is all a 'today's girl' can do and she follows the same protocol.

'You didn't tell me that you have started writing,' Ved says excitedly. He has come to know about something he never heard of in college days.

'You always told me to do so,' she winks at him and laughs.

'I used to say that sarcastically but I am happy that at least you marked my words.'

Ved wants to know more about her writing skills.

'Well, sometimes I do,' she smiles at him, handing over the notebook that he had left on his desk in haste.

'This is news. Writing a book or something?' Ved comes half a step forward in anticipation, though he can only see her attractive profile.

'No, not at all. Just sometimes when I feel like,' she says and pauses. 'Well, some terrible poetry as far as I can remember; I have showed it to you too. That night, remember?'

Ved is horrible at remembering things. She takes him back to the night when Ved and Iona were completely drunk and jumping walls to go up to the terrace of the academic block. They wanted to do something thrilling before leaving college.

Ved was drunk and too stubborn to listen to anyone. Adrika ended up reading some funny poems. Then, the next morning, they all had a tough time at the Dean's office.

'I can't forget that night!' Ved exclaims and claps his hands in joy as he remembers the incident.

'Me too! You almost cried in front of the Dean to save yourself,' Adrika laughs too.

'Why don't you and Arjun write a book together? He already has some female fan following, you will have the male one. You both will rock together,' he giggles sharing this crazy idea.

'You know Arjun better than I do,' she just smiles, and that answered everything. She continues, 'If Arjun had to do this, he would have done it years ago. And I don't think that this male-female idea works, because people need an inspirational story, not a gendered writer.'

'Hmm...no problem, but write a book for sure.'

'Sure, sure. So, is Anushka also coming?' she asks.

'I think so, since Dimpy Aunty does not know where we live. So they both must be coming,' he replies, giving her some irrelevant logic. Dimpy Aunty can reach anywhere even if she has no maps.

♥

Making memories and then sharing them after years strengthens relationships. They make you smile in joyous remembrance, but sometimes they even hurt if you keep thinking about something you never wanted to happen in the past.

In fact, what we expect never always happens in life, because life is a balance of good and bad, and we cannot always expect good things to happen us. That is what Adrika's father used to tell her when she was growing up.

'What are you hiding from me?' Adrika suddenly asks Ved. She has been trying to talk to him since the birthday night, when she saw him teary-eyed, sitting alone in his room before she left.

'Who? Me?' Ved questions her. He pretends to be unaware of anything. But the way he utters the two words together makes it clear to her that he is hiding something from her. Definitely!

'You have changed. You don't discuss things with me now, as you used to in college,' Adrika plays a different card. If Ved does not tell her anything, she may ask Arjun.

'No, nothing like that,' Ved says coolly.

'It is. You just share jokes with me. This is not what we used to be like, were we?' she also emphasizes on her last two words. Words are emotions, she knows well.

'Everyone is busy now. I feel that sharing my problems with you or Arjun may trouble you for no reason,' he smiles, taking the water bottle from her hand and sipping from it.

He has spoken the realism of life, though casually. When we grow up, we do not have the time to listen to our own family or friends—people with whom we created most of the cherished memories. We all become busier and busier.

'Oh, my big boy has become more stupid. That is rubbish, if you think so. You know why I love you guys so much? Because I have seen myself falling down, growing up, then falling down again, and then again rising high with you, Arjun and Iona. I am not being philosophical; we all have responsibilities in life when we grow up but I think we can spare a minute for those who are the most important in our life. No?' she asks, coming a step ahead of him.

Ved smiles, 'Yes, we can.'

'So tell me, what you are hiding from me?' she asks him again.

'Again?'

'I am not going to leave you,' she snatches the water bottle from his hand to make him comfortable so that he shares his feelings with her.

'Nothing! I am cool. Let us go, else we will be late,' Ved takes a few steps and then pauses, realizing that Adrika hasn't moved at all.

'No,' she says, standing like a little girl in the middle of the sideway.

'What happened? Adrika, we are blocking the way,' he takes a step back. Adrika pulls his hand, 'Can we sit somewhere if you allow me and if we are not getting late? Because I am super hungry.'

Without thinking, he says, 'Sure.'

'Okay! Let us sit here,' Adrika looks around for a place to sit. They find an open street café near the college building. She knows if she fails to ask him today, he will become stronger and will not tell her ever again. She is not just smart, but clever too. She knows how and where to use the right skill for the right thing.

Ved approaches the counter to buy a sandwich for her. Adrika leaves her handbag on the bench and stands next to him at the counter.

'Is everything fine with Iona?' she asks.

Ved ignores as if he has not heard her.

Adrika raises her neck, her face is now in front of his face, and asks the same question again.

'Why are you asking this? Did Arjun tell you anything?' Ved probes.

'I didn't ask anyone anything because I thought you would tell me the truth. I saw you at the birthday night. You are hiding something, that I am sure of, but I expect you to tell me what it is. Don't I deserve that?'

'It's not like that…I was the one who enjoyed the most at the birthday party, didn't I?' Ved tries to take the conversation back to a week ago.

'Why have you guys started treating me as if I have met you just a few weeks ago? Okay, no problem I'll not ask again,' she smiles and turns to get back to her seat.

'Wait! Hold this,' he gives her the veg exotic wrap with an iced tea.

'There is nothing to know. We are not together. I lost her.' Ved says with no emotions on his face. His emotions are dry as dust.

When we are in pain, even our small acts define it well. He puts his glass on the table with no interest.

'What?' she almost topples the half-filled glass on the table.

Fourteen

IT WAS JUST a month after the fest when Adrika left college to join her pre-recruitment training. College was not over officially. The last three months changed everything for Ved and Arjun. Ved is one of those men who are stronger physically but weak emotionally. Most men are.

We become possessive about those things we do not want to lose. That emotional weakness made him possessive about Iona.

Everything was going fine between Iona and Ved. One day, he came to know about one of her friends who was a part of the mixed basketball team, of which Iona was the captain.

He started enquiring about her whereabouts. He never stopped her for anything before, but he could not just see, but also feel the change in her. Hate is a four-letter word. So is love. Sometimes we do not understand the difference between the two. Ved became possessive about Iona because she started spending all her time with her friend on the basketball court. As the days passed, they started fighting. It was Christmas evening. Arjun was back home. Iona and Ved were struggling to resolve things between them, and their relationship was on the edge. She got frustrated and filed a case of sexual assault against him. Ved tried to resolve their issues, but everything was so messed up that it ruined their relationship. Ved was rusticated from college for the rest of his exams.

The college authorities requested Iona to withdraw the complaint and Ved, too, pleaded with her as this could ruin his career. Thinking about his mother and younger unmarried sister, Ved swore an affidavit that he would not talk to Iona while they were still in college. Eventually, he stopped talking to everyone. Rumours spread like fire in the college, and everybody came to know that Iona had filed a rape case against Ved. You cannot stop rumours.

That was the worst year of college for Arjun and Ved. Iona stopped talking to Arjun as well because Ved was his roommate and she felt that everything had changed. Their own friends had a different perception of Ved, and this affected Arjun too. Arjun had to face the consequences of the rumours, and was advised by many to leave Ved, else he would ruin his career too. But Arjun knew Ved better. Therefore, he tried to fix things and keep the group together, but all his efforts were in vain. Their equation had changed. It was the last year of college; everyone got jobs through campus placements and left, but this group remained a topic of gossip for their juniors forever.

'This is heart-wrenching and awful. So what now? She did not try…'

Adrika wants to ask more but it is too late. Moreover, it is too late for both of them to resolve the differences.

'Relationships become stronger with time, but sometimes grow weaker with doubts, limits and possessiveness. This is what I have learnt. Arjun told me one thing that day—this is the age of transition; what we become today, we remain so for the rest of our lives. I think, I too have changed and moved on. I still miss her, but I miss only the good times we all had. Let's leave it at that,' Ved says, and does not want to discuss this further. His eyes become moist and gradually fill up with tears. He wipes the tears from his cheeks. This is the first time Adrika has seen him crying. She takes the bottle from his hand, puts it on the other side of the table and says, 'All this happened and Arjun didn't even tell me.' Then she realizes that Ved needs her support rather than have her regretting something that happened in the past.

'We all have a past but it should not become a daunting baggage and spill over to the present,' Adrika holds his hand and assures him that Arjun and she cannot replace the memories he had with Iona but they are always there for him when he needs them.

She feels his pain and knows that if she cries, he will cry more. Girls are kind and emotional by nature, but they can definitely show their strength when it is required. That is what Ved needs now. Ved takes her hand in his hands. Life is all about holding hands and for long, he has just realized.

'Life is so difficult to live, so painful to survive and so bitter to know about, and now…I am so lonely. I miss my good times,' he says and bursts into tears.

There is complete silence around and words have become more effective and painful.

'Don't cry,' says Adrika, coming closer on the table and wiping his tears. When she touches his cheeks to wipe the tears, it reminds him of the times when Iona used to do the same to kiss.

'Yeah, I am fine,' says Ved. 'Actually we have grown up, so we really don't cry.' With these few words, he buries his head in his hands and rocks back and forth, sobbing as he does so, the tears streaming down his face. He presses his lips together for a while before looking back at Adrika.

'It's not like that…' says Adrika. This is the only response we manage to muster when we do not have anything else to say.

'Everyone used to cheer me up when I performed well on the ground, but nobody came to me when I was in pain. Nobody. Not even my friends whom I had trusted the most.

That is what life is.'

He sits quietly, his arms wrapped tightly around himself, looking down and waiting for the tears to dry up.

It is often said that we should not break the thread of love; if broken, it cannot be put back together, except with a knot. Adrika recalls the days she spent with Iona and the others. Everything Ved has told her about Iona has changed her perception.

'It happens in life. You yourself say that some relations make good memories and some lessons.'

'I have lost in life. I did everything and...'

'Whatever happened, could have happened to anyone. It happened to me too. It takes time but things will turn on your side.' Before he stands up, she gets up to stand in front of him. She touches his chin, pulls it up a bit, and looks into his bloodshot, wet eyes. She hugs him tightly. This makes their bond stronger, which has been that way always.

'Now let us go, else Hitler will shout at us at home,' Ved says getting up.

She laughs louder than usual and that makes him laugh too.

♥

On their way, Adrika combs her hair and quickly puts gloss on her lips to make them look fresh and lively.

Do all girls do this? Probably, they do.

Ved pinches his cheeks. He has seen Arjun doing it to give himself a natural look and instant make-up.

Adrika is the simplest among her friends. As a warning, Dimpy Aunty is a great lie detector. She is an expert in profiling people. Probably a layer of gloss will help.

When she is being sweet to Arjun, she even appreciates

the extra salty daal cooked by Arjun. Sometimes Arjun helps her in cooking too. This is something that his mother does not like at all. He does not lie to his mom, and so they just end up having arguments.

Habitually, on weekends, Arjun and Ved spend time at her home. They say that though their mothers have given them birth, but the humour they have, has come from the dinner table conversations with Dimpy Aunty, with extra curd and butter on the side.

Today it is quite the opposite...

Ved rings the bell.

The door opens and Dimpy Aunty greets them. Ved has started following Arjun. These actions are called precautions before the explosion, if any. He greets her by touching her feet.

'Where is Arjun?' Adrika asks, dropping her bag on the sofa. She is poised and calm.

'Aunty she is Adrika, Adrika, she is our mother,' Ved winks at Dimpy Aunty.

'How are you, beta?'

'I am good, Aunty. We are college friends. Now I work in Mumbai...' Adrika says while greeting her. Arjun and Anushka appear from the kitchen. Adrika passes a smile and waves.

'Good! At least they have someone sensible in the league,' Dimpy Aunty answers. Sometimes it looks like she only makes fun of Arjun and Ved. Probably she loves them a lot.

They sit around the dining table waiting for Arjun to present the exotic self-cooked meal of the day.

♥

'What happened to your arms?' Anushka pushes her chair back and comes closer to examine Adrika's shoulder.

Did she just see a love bite? The thought scared Adrika. She looks at her arms to find the blue and brown spots on her shoulder and arms. She becomes conscious and tries to hide them right away.

'What happened?' Arjun knows her very well. She can hide things for years without discussing. He examines again, 'How did you get these?' They do not look like love bites, he knows that. Adrika faces a dilemma; she neither wants to hide nor is she confident enough to tell them that she is in a relationship. She is meeting Dimpy Aunty for the first time. Definitely, not a good idea. It will be stupid to share this in her presence.

'Did somebody hurt you?' Ved asks in alarm. She gazes at Dimpy Aunty.

'No,' she replies instantly.

'Where did you get those?' Arjun enquires. If she does not want to tell, that is all right with him. However, he does not want her to hide anything from him.

Adrika shrugs, 'Chill! I fell in the washroom last week. I was sleepy and didn't realize there was water on the floor and slipped.'

'You can put something on it, it will go away. These marks never stay on the body,' Arjun responds looking into her eyes, trying hard to know if she is speaking the truth or telling a lie.

She smiles widely at Arjun. He does not respond and retreats to the kitchen. He wants to call her aside and ask what has happened. Adrika follows him, pretending that she needs something, 'Hey Arjun, can you give me a glass of water?'

Before she reaches the refrigerator, she feels a tug on her shoulder. She turns around and finds Arjun hot on her heels.

'What are you hiding behind this devilish smile?' Arjun asks casually. He knows if she has decided not to tell him, then she will not share it with anybody.

'Arjun chill! Nothing has happened. Stop using your mind unnecessarily. You will get nothing,' Adrika blinks at him and adds, 'Should I help you in cooking?' She looks mysterious when she blinks.

'Yes, let me see how you cook,' Arjun gives her a knife to chop onions. He just concentrates on her profile. Sometimes, even temporary wrinkles say more than words. He gets his answer. He comes to the hall where everyone is chit-chatting and enjoying the company of Dimpy Aunty. She is cracking jokes and making everyone laugh.

Anushka looks at Arjun, asking something without words.

'Nothing,' Arjun gestures.

Adrika has decided to tell them once Aunty leaves. She does not want to hide it any longer. She started feeling uncomfortable since the day Sumrit asked her why she was hiding their relationship from her friends. She told him that she was waiting for the right time. *Today* is the right time. Vibration on the table and beeps of her cell phone break the silence. She has received a WhatsApp message. One of her colleagues confirmed her relocation to Bengaluru. She has been trying hard not to go, but now she has to leave by next Monday.

'Hey, Arjun I have to leave,' she whispers into his ears.

Aunty notices. She does not ignore small things.

'What happened? Anything serious?' Arjun asks her

'Nothing. I will see you people tomorrow evening if I leave early from office. I am probably moving to Bengaluru next week. So, let's meet before I leave,' she says.

'But you have been here for only a couple of months,' Arjun says.

'Yeah, I have completed my probation period, so…time to go,' she smiles. The fake smile.

'Dinner?' Anushka asks.

'Still have some time,' she blinks and gets up to say bye.

'Take care of yourself, you have to bear me a long way,' Adrika says to Ved, as if she is sharing some secret. She pats him on his shoulder.

'Thanks!' Ved just smiles. Probably they both have spoken through their eyes.

Adrika leaves.

Fifteen

THERE IS NO reason to party, as Adrika does not want to leave this city. This place has given her the time she needed to reunite with old friends, and the numerous good and some odd memories. She does not want to remember the odd ones. Life cannot be perfect all the time. Therefore, she has tried to forget the ruthless times she had when she was new to the city. Now, leaving everyone again after college is little tougher. If she had the option, she would have definitely stayed back in Mumbai.

Adrika is a modern Indian girl who is emotional but not weak. She is one of those girls who know that it isn't the end of the world when a boy takes too long to answer her text or opens their snaps without replying or cancels plans at the last second. She knows that it doesn't matter how many dates she gets asked out on or how many likes she gets on an attractive picture she posts. She understands that it's okay if she has been hurt in past but she tries hard so that that does not happen in the future. Undoubtedly, she has become smarter and self-dependent, has found ways to manage her life and friends, and will not surrender easily to situations—no matter what comes her way.

She works hard. She manages things. She respects people. She knows her traditions. Yes, these girls exist. Adrika is one of them.

Adrika has decided to make her departure a little thrilling and exciting with a news that will shock everyone. The thought of how everyone will react is making her a little nervous.

Keeping social status and ethics aside, Adrika has thrown a party, but not at a restaurant. She has chosen a dhaba this time to celebrate before she leaves the city. Many a times, little gestures bring in good times. Perhaps, spending time at a roadside dhaba will be one of them for everyone. She has invited everyone to a dhaba, far away from the town.

She must have some plans, though she is bad at making them. Arjun is the one who ends up doing everything. He is that shoulder to put one's gun and fire. That poor boy!

♥

It is almost midnight with a cold breeze blowing and petrichor wafting in the air. Thatched shacks with the roofs held up with bamboo poles with a few chairs, tables and long wooden benches and cots all around in the open area give the area a great ambience.

Cool air and twinkling stars, entwined with the smell of mud tandoor... This is going to be the best trip ever. However, Arjun is bothered about his next day's work. He didn't want to come on this short trip. He has come because he does not want to give them a chance to say that he has changed.

'What if it rains? I was telling you all, let's take a cab,' Arjun is worried of hypothetical scenarios... the 'What ifs?'

'Why do you always think of the future?' Anushka, sitting next to him, says softly so that only Arjun can hear. She has changed him from an introvert to an extrovert. However, sometimes she finds his older symptoms returning, but resolves them with her smile and logic. Making someone understand things is as important as understanding things yourself. Anushka has the sense of knowing Arjun and she knows well which pulse she has to put her finger on. Perhaps, she will be a good dominating partner one day just like her mother. Arjun should definitely end this friendship with a proposal. No other woman can face his tantrums.

Before he speaks anything, Adrika joins in, 'She is right. We will see if it rains. I am sure he is worried about us and not the weather.'

'Isn't it?' Ved comes into the confab. Arjun nods in agreement, 'Okay, okay.'

Adrika sits on the extreme left, leaving some space next to her, in front of Arjun and Anushka. Arjun is on the extreme right on the spacious cot.

It looks like Ved and Adrika are teaming up. They begin cracking jokes. It is easy for them to make fun of Arjun today.

In the background, a cook is preparing naans and chicken in a mud tandoor. A couple of boys are serving the customers. A few trucks have been parked around the dhaba with their drivers and attendants catching a snooze. A thin boy appears to take their order.

'I want palm wine (taadi),' Adrika jumps up.

'Same here,' Ved says.

'No hard drinks,' Arjun says with restrictive eyes.

'Yes, guys, no drinks. You guys need to go home as well, no drinks,' Anushka supports him. Probably she does not want to drink. Arjun is worried about dropping everyone home safely, as always.

'It's fun, let's have some shots of palm wine,' Adrika pleads. Her feelings are visible on her face, she will not let go of this chance. Arjun rarely says no to Adrika; he always gives her the space that she deserves to have fun in life. Today, she has all the right.

'No, it's not your hotel, it's a dhaba,' Arjun says in a firm disapproval.

'It's okay, just one. We have come all the way here. Without hookah and palm wine, holy spirits will curse us,' Ved says.

'I am not going to be responsible for anyone,' Arjun says and lets them order whatever they want to. However, Arjun must be ready with their travel plan after that.

They order palm wine.

♥

'So here is the deal,' Adrika says, having some exciting plan in her mind, before the order arrives on the table.

'And what's that?' asks Anushka. A man comes and keeps two bottles of palm wine and four glasses on the table between the two cots. He starts pouring while Arjun busies himself on his phone. Sometimes Arjun is very annoying.

Ved snatches the phone from his hand and keeps in it the pocket of his jacket. Before Arjun questions anything, Ved answers with his expressions.

'As this is my last night out with you guys, I don't want to let it go without making it memorable...'

'Right,' Arjun nods.

'What? So that's confirmed?' Anushka asks.

'Yeah. I have told Arjun and Ved about it. That's why I wanted to meet you all. I really do not want to leave you guys, but...'

'That's okay; it's not that far away that you can't come visit us. You can definitely come over the weekends,' Ved adds.

Adrika says, 'Hopefully, well, I have something to ask. Everyone has to share their secrets with each small sip of the wine, or finish the glass in one go if you don't want to be an open book today. I know we all have secrets. I am not expecting anybody to be a loser.'

'I can tell Arjun's secrets on behalf of him,' Ved laughs and Anushka follows.

'Not bad, what say?' Anushka winks looking at Arjun. She knows he has many but he never discloses.

'I have no secrets,' Arjun replies with a smile—the notorious smile which has kept so many secrets hidden.

'L-O-L...look, who is talking,' Ved laughs aloud.

'No, I mean we all have secrets, but not important ones,' he defends himself.

'No, this is for me and you can't say no,' Adrika says.

'Do not be a spoilsport,' Ved puts fuel to the fire.

'Maybe he is too shy to share a secret,' Adrika says in fun.

'Not at all.'

Arjun raises his glass up. Others follow.

'Cheers to life.'

'Cheers to friendship.'

'Let us do everything in life—good and bad—together. Good will give us memories to cherish. Bad will teach us new lessons.'

'Let us not tell the things that we have done so far. Not even to our future partners. They will judge us for no reason. We don't.'

'Let us leave our souls free and take an oath that secrets will remain secrets outside of this place.'

They cheer with a clink of shots.

♥

Ved takes the first sip.

'Ved, there you go, but you have to sip it once if you are willing to share a secret, and gulp it all down if you aren't,' Adrika points out. Ved understands.

'No! I was just checking.' He takes a sip, and says, 'One

of my secrets is that I once cried bitterly in front of Iona just to get her sympathy during a fight, and then everything was solved. However, it only worked for a few fights because I started doing it too often. So, I had to find another way.'

They laugh.

'So mean! You...' Adrika murmurs.

'Now, Arjun...' Anushka says in excitement, thinking how Arjun will finish his wine in one go. Arjun smells it.

'No, that's not allowed,' Adrika stops him. Nevertheless, Arjun puts the glass to his lips, tilts his head back, and gulps the wine down until the last drop.

'Pass,' he says.

'Ooooo...' everyone says.

'Yay! He is the dark horse,' Ved shouts. People sitting faraway look at them.

'That's not done, Arjun. You are ruining the game,' Adrika says.

'You guys are making your own rules now. Okay, okay, do not cry. So...one of my secrets is that I haven't smoked in my life.'

'That's not a secret, that's a habit!' Anushka interrupts.

'Yes, no cheating,' Anushka says.

Adrika nodded, 'Yes.'

'Cheating? See who is going against the rules of the game now. Okay, I have a fear of the dark. When Ved was out of town, I came out of the house and spent the whole night in the park. A light beam on the front wall behind the dancing tree kept me alive. Trust me, it was scary.'

'Whole night...seriously?' Adrika tries to control her laughter.

Arjun looks a little embarrassed.

'Now don't judge me,' Arjun replies and continues, 'Now you go.' He points to Anushka.

Anushka promptly raises her glass high and takes a big sip.

'Remember, a secret,' Arjun reminds her.

'Yeah, yeah. Mom and my sister Angira know most of the secrets that Arjun has shared with me so far. That itself is a secret, no?'

'What? All?' Arjun is stunned recollecting all the rubbish things he did and told Anushka.

'That's why Dimpy Aunty always flares up when she meets you,' Ved laughs.

'Chill! All your secrets are funny, do not be serious about it,' Anushka clarifies.

'A few were never supposed to be shared,' laments Arjun. Poor Arjun looks helpless. It seems as if this night out is not working out very well for him.

'Well, what's the secret of Arjun?' Ved reminds Anushka.

'Seems like you guys had planned this game to target only me, go on,' says Arjun.

'Okay,' Anushka relaxes and says, 'So, he has a fear of turbulence and once, because of this fear, he had cancelled his flight.'

'That's not a secret,' Arjun interrupts, 'My mom told me to cancel it because it was raining really hard in Mumbai.'

'Don't lie, don't lie. Mom and Angira told me about it,' Anushka reveals.

'Hold on, hold on,' Adrika downs the remaining alcohol in her glass, but cringes a little as she does not like its taste. She is trying out palm wine for the first time. Despite that she finishes it in one go.

'So...?' Ved asks her the moment she keeps her glass down.

'Yes, so the first secret of my life is that I haven't been to any dance class. I learnt most of the steps under the shower.'

'You are cheating again. This is not a secret. Arjun also did that,' Anushka says.

Arjun looks at Anushka.

'Sorry,' she hums at him.

Stopping others from giggling, Adrika continues, 'Okay, okay! So let me make it more interesting. Since I have not lied to you guys ever in my life, I need to tell you that I am in a relationship with someone.'

'What?'

The first word comes from Arjun.

'Yes. I decided to tell you guys before I moved to Bengaluru,' Adrika replies and waits for them to change their reactions.

'So I was right that day?' Arjun tries to connect all the dots. Adrika answers with a nod.

'What's his name?' Ved asks her.

'Sumrit.'

'Yeah. Your friend. He is a nice guy,' Adrika says, expecting Arjun to respond.

'Sumrit?' Ved asks in amusement.

'Yeah.'

'Congratulations! You could have asked him to come too,' Anushka looks happy for her.

'Congratulations!' Ved says with a smile.

However, Ved does not look as happy as she expected him to be. Maybe he hoped to be the first person to know about it. Arjun carries the same reaction as Ved.

'Thanks!' Adrika says while looking at Arjun. She takes her cell phone out and messages him on WhatsApp.

I am sorry. I was about to tell you long ago but I was waiting for the right time.

But I love you more than anybody else

Arjun takes his phone back from Ved and taps to reply.

> That's Okay :)
> Happy for you.

♥

The moon struggles to shine through the thick clouds that have covered the sky. The clouds hang like tattered grey curtains, framing an inky indigo sky. Without all the city lights, one can see the stars twinkling and winking at people on Earth. Time flies like it always does when you are having fun, and it is already 12.45 a.m.

'So, when will you settle down and start to feel jealous of us partying?' Ved tries to mock her. Many times in life, what you like and what you do not, do not decide others' happiness; rather, your happiness lies in others' contentment. That is the sign of maturity. Ved has become a mature person.

Although Ved does not like Sumrit, maybe because they have been captains of opponent teams, he is glad to see Adrika happy after a long time. Love changes everything—sometimes it weaves unforgettable memories, while sometimes it teaches us a lesson.

They all wish her to have a great future.

Adrika smiles at Ved, and they talk without uttering a word.

'When are you moving to Bengaluru?' Arjun asks her and immediately shoots another question, 'But he is doing his MBA, right?'

'I have to join office next Monday. Yes, he will be here.' She smiles. It is going to be difficult to manage a long-distance relationship, but Adrika has managed everything so far.

'Thanks so much, you all. Next party in Bengaluru,' she adds.

'We'll wait for you to come back. Should we leave?' Arjun questions them. Ensuring a timely departure after partying has been a task for him. Especially, when drunken Ved is with them.

All of them get up while Adrika pays the bill. With warm hugs and lots of fun, Adrika takes the good memories of the last trip in Mumbai with her.

Sixteen

SOMETIMES, EXPRESSING OUR pain in words hurts more because subconsciously it brings back everything without letting us know. The conversation with Adrika reminds Ved of everything once again. Adrika should not have asked him about the worst time he has gone through.

Early morning on a weekend, Ved wakes up and feels the darkness around him.

The more you think about negative things and run away from pain, they come back in the same form and hurt more. You have to play with your mind before it weakens you emotionally.

Ved senses the darkness around him and fears that it will soon swallow him. An aura of grey and a mist that will not lift surrounds him.

He checks Arjun's room twice in the last few minutes. Finding him asleep, he finds solace in his last cigarette, which will not eradicate his pain, but will give him strength to dissolve it temporarily. Standing at the window of the hall, he lights the cigarette. If Ajrun and Ved have ever fought or argued, they have always done so over his smoking and drinking habits, which he has started again in the last couple of weeks.

Everything seems to be collapsing on him. He has not discussed anything with Arjun in the last couple of months as Arjun has his own struggles to deal with. He does not want to be a burden. Arjun has already tried to make him understand that it will take time. And one day, everything *will* be alright.

Ved is going through a rough phase. Those memories with Iona have again started haunting him at nights. He was the one who captained a football team in college, but is failing to take control of his life today and feels like a loser in pain. Sometimes, our own situations weaken us gradually, until we are completely broken.

Hiding his pain, he keeps his tears hidden behind his eyelids.

He is not yet out of that trauma, when his mother calls him to inform that things are not good at home. There have been some property issues for the last few months. Ved tells Arjun about it. His uncle has taken everything when his grandmother passed away. Now his sister and mother have received a legal notice to vacate their place in a month.

'Ved, what are you doing? The doctor has told you strictly to not smoke and you have started again!' Arjun takes the cigarette from his hand and throws it out of the window.

Yesterday he had thrown up and the doctor had advised him to quit drinking and smoking.

Arjun is worried about him because he is not recovering and things are getting worse.

'What? What happened? Why did you throw it? That was the last one,' Ved says irately.

'Because…you had stopped smoking and the doctor told you not to smoke!' Arjun shouts at him.

Ved has always been there for Arjun in his bad times and now Arjun cannot leave Ved alone even if he does not like his words. There are a few things we do without thinking about their consequences.

'Chill! Nothing will happen to me,' Ved says as if Arjun has done something wrong to him.

'Yes, that I can see. 'Do you know what you are doing to yourself?' Arjun raises his voice a little louder.

He repeats when Ved does not answer his question but keeps staring outside the window.

'Things will be fine,' Arjun sits next to him.

Arjun also knows that he cannot do anything. In fact, nobody can. It takes a lot of time to come out of the situation Ved is going through. We only support things on social media, in movies, or books, but reality exists behind the walls. Only a few people come in to comfort you during the ruthless times. Arjun changes the topic to divert his mind and asks, 'What did Aunty say about the notice?'

♥

'Nothing, they need to leave the house as of now, and then we need to file a case in the court,' Ved replies. When we hit a rough patch, all problems come together to test us.

'Let us invite your sister and Aunty here for some days. They will also feel good,' Arjun suggests, trying to distract Ved, as lately he has started thinking negatively about himself—that he was good for nothing.

'I just want to finish my MBA, get a job in the States, and leave this country. At least nobody will judge me and my family,' Ved says and walks back to his room.

'Ved, it happens. Things will be fine for sure. We just need to wait.'

'I cannot see my family homeless, right? You want me to wait rather than giving me a solution?' Ved shouts at him.

His irritation is evident in his words. Arjun ignores it because he knows Ved's situation.

Arjun takes a few steps towards Ved and holds his shoulder. They both pause. Ved turns and the two friends hug each other. Ved needed this...he has been lonely for so long.

When we are in trouble, we know people cannot solve our problems, even the ones close to us. But we do need those people to provide us with a shoulder to cry on and to make us believe that we are not weak.

'What did I do wrong in my life? Why I am suffering? I did not do anything wrong to anyone,' Ved can hide anything behind his eyes. However, he cannot pretend anymore. He bursts into tears.

'I did everything for Iona. She left me. What should I do?' he sniffs and pours his heart out to Arjun.

'Things will be fine. You can trust me...hmm?' Arjun consoles him keeping his hand on his shoulder. A few pats and some love may change something. They argue over small things and fight over different views, but they always end up standing by each other's side.

'It's difficult to live like this,' Ved says, wiping his tears.

'Call Aunty and your sister, and book their tickets. Everything will be fine when they will meet Dimpy Aunty,' Arjun tries to make him smile and pokes on his ribs.

'Hmm…'

'Yes, what say?' Arjun understands his mood swings and has become proficient in handling them. Arjun pats on his back one more time to boost his mood up.

'…and she will tell everything to my mom, too, just like she did to yours,' releasing himself, Ved smiles and continues, 'I was also thinking of calling them here,' Ved says in agreement.

'Now let's go, Adrika is leaving today and she has already called twice,' Arjun says looking at his wristwatch.

'I want to come but I have to call Mom,' Ved goes to open his cupboard.

Arjun picks up his phone, realizes that he will be late picking up Adrika from her place, and then dropping her at the airport before she misses her flight.

♥

'I didn't know guys also take hours to get ready. I am travelling, not you. All you have to do is come and drop me at the airport. If you do not want to come, it is okay. I just wanted to meet you for the last time,' Adrika splurts out. Her outbursts are on priority.

Arjun was not expecting her call because many things change when you are in a relationship. However, Adrika messaged him last night saying that Sumrit had gone to his home town in Solan.

'Hey, I am sorry. I am ready. Actually, Ved had some urgent work, so it took time. Leaving in a minute, and stop showing your tantrums. I am reaching there,' blaming Ved for the delay, Arjun keeps himself safe if she misses her flight.

However, it will not take much time for the 'if' to turn into surety if he does not reach soon.

'Arjun, I'll miss my flight,' Adrika says like she is neither excited nor sad. She is numb about her departure to Bengaluru. She will definitely miss the time she spent in Mumbai with Sumrit, Arjun, Ved and Anushka.

'Don't worry, you won't miss us,' Arjun responds, tying his shoelaces, sitting on the sofa in the hall. Ved comes into the hall holding a beautifully wrapped gift box, 'Give it to her and tell her we will all meet soon.'

'What's in this?' Arjun asks curiously.

'This is not for you, so don't you dare open it. Tell her to open this once she reaches Bengaluru,' Ved says.

'Okay! I won't.'

He waves at Ved and leaves.

♥

Taking shortcuts that Arjun has never tried before, they reach the airport.

'I always used to think that life becomes chilled out and stress-free after college,' Adrika says by the time they reach the airport.

'Yes, it's not. You have duties to drop friends at the airport without even having breakfast,' Arjun says, pulling her bags.

'Sarcasm?' Adrika takes a few chocolates out from her pocket and gives them to him, 'You can have these.'

'You have more than an hour. I was telling you, we will not get late,' Arjun states confidently.

'Now you look more confident. You could have said the same thing to boost my confidence when we were stuck in traffic too, couldn't you?' Adrika shows what tangible sarcasm is.

'Even if you miss the flight, you can catch a direct bus to Bengaluru.'

'Oh! But big people. They don't travel in buses.' He continues teasing her, as he knows she cannot travel in buses. She gets sick.

'Just like you love commuting via flights and that too in turbulence. Dimpy Aunty was telling me the other day about your Chandigarh trip. Remember?' Adrika chokes him.

'Everyone in this world has some fear,' Arjun says defending himself.

'Exactly, everyone has some problem with something or the other, right?' she smiles.

Never have an argument with a girl. You will end up sealing your lips or with an embarrassing smile.

'Let's go.' Adrika pulls his hand to navigate him towards the open café outside the airport entrance, without expecting any reply from him.

Arjun unwraps a chocolate and takes a giant bite. An empty stomach needs one.

'We can sit here and then I can leave. I wanted to talk to you about something,' Adrika offers him a chair.

♥

'Yeah, you want something?' Arjun turns to the counter to get something to eat.

'No, I don't. I cannot eat early in the morning,' Adrika says while texting Sumrit about her departure.

Arjun buys his favourite veg Lebanese wrap.

'So what did you want to talk about?' Arjun asks her as he sits down on the chair.

'What has happened to Ved?' she asks without giving any overview.

'What happened?' Arjun asks her as if he does not know anything or maybe he does not want Adrika to know about anything.

'Iona and Ved were the best together, no?' Adrika asks expecting an affirmative reply from him. However, time changes. So do we.

'They were,' he mumbles and takes a big bite of the wrap, which gives him an excuse to pause.

'But...'

'It was a bad time for me too. Let us not talk about that. You want a bite?' Arjun offers her the wrap and completely ignores her words because he has also gone through the same phase of disrespect that Ved did.

'It's okay. How's he now?' She does not know that the problems have still not left his side, though emotionally.

'He is fighting and recovering. He talks about you a lot but you have Sumrit, so…' Arjun changes the topic.

'Talks about me?'

'Yeah, but he understands that someone is there to share your time.'

She leans a bit forward and comes closer to the table.

'By the way, when are you proposing to Anushka?' she randomly asks him something that he does not even know himself.

With the progression of time tending to her departure, she wants to know everything about everyone.

'Don't know,' Arjun retorts.

'Why?'

'I haven't been that lucky in love. So sometimes, I get scared. What if I tell her, or Dimpy Aunty, and she says no?'

'Nobody is lucky; we all have both sides of life—good and bad. You have kept everything well and managed so far in life, it should not be difficult for you to decide, right?' Adrika is very smart. She keeps asking for confirmation to her statements. First love changes everyone because it is all about emotions. When we find it the second time, we become mature. Still, Arjun is scared of losing people.

'Then what's the solution?' asks Adrika.

'I can be with her being her best friend until she realizes that I am the right one for her,' Arjun grins.

'Isn't that the very traditional way?'

'Maybe, but this is required as of now,' he smirks again.

'Well, Aunty is right…'

'Who? Dimpy Aunty?' he questions.

She laughs and adds, 'Yes, she was saying the other day

that you have grown up and become mature.'

'Sometimes the sun rises from the West, nice. Well, I am sure she saw a few strands of grey hair on my right cheek. So she meant I have become mature.' He laughs.

She laughs out loud, 'That's height of negativity. Come out of it. She is nice.'

'Someone is hypnotized.'

'Chill! Now let's go,' Adrika checks her watch and pulls her bags together.

'Yeah,' Arjun walks with her towards the entry gate.

'I'll miss you guys. Say hi to Ved and Anushka,' she says, skipping the name of Iona and pretending it does not matter to her.

It matters a lot to her. Iona and Adrika were 4 a.m. friends. Sometimes you have to be on one side. Maybe, she had chosen the right one.

'Give my love to Dimpy Aunty and Mom,' she adds and blinks.

Arjun gives her a heartfelt hug without being emotional. This is what he has learnt to be over the years.

She waves. He waves back, and then she disappears behind the giant pillars and the crowd.

Seventeen

THE WEATHER IS pleasant in Bengaluru. It is almost as if nature is setting up the perfect ambience for a meeting for Adrika and Sumrit. Sumrit wants to give Adrika a surprise, so he has come to Bengaluru to meet her and help her settle down in the city.

Surprises bring a lot of joy. However, exceptions are always there. Sumrit is standing at the reception of the hotel he has booked. It seems it is not his day.

'Sir if you have any identity proof or something, we can allow you both because it's strictly mentioned in our policies that unmarried couples are not allowed to book a room together,' a big man at the reception says. Sumrit gives him a non-appreciative look.

The receptionist points out to an old laminated pamphlet, 'See, it is the order by the Commissioner.'

Men in South India are generally sweet and nice but destiny has set some exceptions today; he looks strict. 'We were engaged and just last month we got married. How can I have a marriage certificate or something to show you?' Sumrit says confidently. Being confident makes the wrong things right, he has learnt this from his college viva. He tries more ways to convince the man. But fails.

'Sir I agree, but without an identity proof we cannot do anything. Hope you understand,' his expressions convey that he is strict and will stick to his words. Holy fathers have said where straightforwardness has never a chance of working, crookedness flourishes.

'Do you have your marriage certificate right now with you?' he asks. 'Who carries the certificate?' Sumrit looks annoyed and says bluntly. He wished it were a female manager; he could have made her agree. They understand love and emotions, unlike this man. Meanwhile, he realizes that overreacting can lead the man into suspicion.

He smiles.

'Wait! She must be on the way. Let me check with her if she is carrying any identity proof of us,' he says and excuses himself for a minute.

He calls Adrika. She must be on the way to the hotel.

'There is a problem,' Sumrit says.

'What happened?' Adrika asks.

'They need proof that we are a married couple.'

'What? Seriously?'

'Yes, they don't allow unmarried couples to stay,' he lowers his voice.

'You didn't check this under hotel policies while booking?' Adrika asks as if she knew everything.

'I checked, but all the hotels had the same condition. Therefore, I thought, they will allow us, but they are saying they will not. Do you have any identity proof with you?'

'Everyone has one if they are not a terrorist, don't they? They need the marriage certificate, right? Now what to do?'

'Leave it, I will go back. We will come some other day,' Sumrit sounds dejected and unhappy.

'That's not fair. At least meet me. We can meet outside and then you can go back,' Adrika wants to meet him. He has come all way to meet her and she was excited at the prospect of meeting him.

'No, I will go and we will meet the next time. Mumbai is much better. I will not come here again. You come to Mumbai,' Sumrit says in frustration. He must have planned things, but one man changed everything.

'Some hotels may not allow,' says Adrika, still thinking about a solution.

'Hmm.'

'Hmm' is the word when you do something wrong and have no excuse to defend yourself. Sumrit should have checked the terms and conditions before booking the hotel.

'Wait! I will do something. I will call you in ten minutes,' Adrika says as if she has a mission to accomplish.

When there is a problem, there is he—Arjun.

♥

We start caring more when people go away. Arjun answers her phone call instantly.

'Hello! How is my dark chocolate?' He has started teasing her by that name from the day she began working as a chocolate taster.

'I am good. And don't be racist,' Adrika chuckles.

He laughs, 'Okay, okay. Have you reached? Where are you?'

'Just on the way. Well, I need your help,' she says immediately without wasting any time.

'I cognize your words well. What happened?' Arjun guesses that she may need contacts of his friends who live in Bengaluru.

'I need a marriage certificate,' Adrika tells him, as if he is the Registrar of State Authority.

'What?'

'Yes, I need it right now,' she says.

He interrupts, 'Why do you need a marriage certificate?

Neither are you married nor can I give you one,' Arjun senses Adrika is going to commit some major mistake. She has done some in college days. No doubt she is sensible, but she is notorious for taking risks too.

'I know but you are good with Photoshop, you can make one for me,' Adrika says, her voice barely audible in the crowded bus. A man sitting next to her looks at her.

'What? Are you mad? And why do you need a marriage certificate?' Arjun probes again. Stepping out of his workplace before someone listens to his unethical conversation, Arjun looks at a signboard while walking towards the break area—*Trust your instincts and your own ability to gauge a situation.* He finds one more next to it—*To be a contributor to your family, work and community, think in terms of 'we' instead of 'I'*.

Probably these two quotes will indirectly help Adrika to brainwash him. Not just holy fathers, but holy mothers have also said that when you want something, the entire universe conspires in helping you achieve it.

'I am not going to do that,' Arjun refuses.

'I am not going to use it for any wrong reasons. Actually, Sumrit has come to Bengaluru and booked a hotel room for us. But they need a marriage certificate, else they will not let us in,' Adrika talks like a roller coaster. Arjun takes time to reply.

'Adrika! I do not think that it's right,' Arjun does not want to help her in this matter.

'Please! Do something. He is standing there and arguing,' Adrika begs.

'Are you sure?' he asks her as if he wanted to hear a 'no'.

'Yeah. You have done this in college days.'

'I am asking about staying in a hotel. Are you sure you want to do this?'

'Yes.'

'I know you are the best person to take the right decisions. There is no problem spending time with the person you love, but relationships take time to grow and there are many things to know about each other. So…' Arjun tells Adrika what he forgot to tell her on the night out when she told everyone about Sumrit.

'Why don't you show them your pics with Sumrit, if you have any?' Arjun still does not feel like doing the illicit work. What if? Sometimes 'what ifs' are important.

'If it could work, then I would have done that. Please help or suggest an alternative.'

Now Arjun realizes why smart people do wrong things. They don't do them by choice; they do them by force.

'Okay, but stay silent and don't do anything stupid. I am not going to be responsible for it,' he warns her.

Arjun looks around while he realizes that his colleagues are looking at him.

'Okay, I will try.'

'Thanks so much.'

♥

By hook or by crook, Adrika and Sumrit check in to the hotel room in the evening after spending more than enough time at the reception. South Indian men are nice. The fact maintains its commitment. Moreover, the auspicious thread around her neck has helped them and played a vital role to make him believe that they are indeed married.

They will stay at the hotel for a day or two before Adrika joins her new office after the weekend.

'Thanks for coming,' Adrika says as she sits on the bed and relaxes. Sumrit nods while looking at the mangalsutra. She feels it looks good on her. When you love a person, everything that connects the two people together becomes more special. Removing it diligently, she keeps it in her handbag. Every relationship has complications, but that itself has encouraged her to give it her best in any situation. The thought emerges when she finds the pieces of the note she kept, for no good reason, safely in her bag. She pushes them deeper into the corner. Lies are okay if used to avoid arguments. She has learnt that over a period.

She takes a box out of her handbag. 'By the way, I have brought something for you,' she says, surprising Sumrit. He smells of fresh soap after a quick bath.

'What is that?' he looks at her and takes the box from her hand curiously.

She tickles his navel. Tickling will not challenge his excitement. Sumrit takes a step back. Ignoring everything happening around, he asks about the box, 'What's in this box?'

'You check.' She hangs on to his shoulder, throwing his towel to the other side of the bed.

'Okay, that's like a surprise,' Sumrit unboxes it and wraps the ribbons around her neck. He finds different kinds of chocolates in the box. Sumrit loves them all.

'These are so nice…you made them?' he asks though he already knows it.

'These are not just chocolates. There is something more to them,' Adrika looks at him, waiting for a question. She spent half a day making these before she left for Bengaluru. Even a small deed makes people happy when you do it out of love. That happiness is evident on her jubilant face.

'Then?' surprisingly, he asks the obvious question.

'I have made them for you, and every chocolate has its own importance. Try a few bites of each,' she urges. She deserves an appreciation. No girl does everything for everyone. They only do it for one person. That is love.

'That's so nice of you,' Sumrit pushes her on the bed.

He approaches to kiss her on the lips and feels the warmth of her body. She has become playful and is not distracted by his body. She pushes him and wants him to stop so that he can concentrate on the chocolates.

'Not now,' she says.

With a sudden thrust and pursed lips, Sumrit gets up and takes one chocolate from the box.

'Okay,' he says.

'Not this one. Pick the first one,'

There is a series of chocolates. Love makes you creative.

'Oh, there is a sequence!' Sumrit looks more excited, and it seems to distract his attention from her splendour.

He unwraps the chocolate, puts the entire thing in his mouth and starts munching. Adrika laughs.

'What happened?' he says, but a moment later he realizes there is something in his mouth.

'You need to take that out, I am sorry,' Adrika says, still giggling.

Sumrit finds a small note. 'What's this?' he asks in curiosity.

'See for yourself.' She expects him to proceed.

Sumrit finds something written on it. It says, 'You make me feel that I don't need anybody else to love me. Will you marry me?'

Sumrit hugs her, murmuring into her ears, 'I love you to the moon and back.'

Definitely, a few drops of tears roll down her cheeks and fall on his shoulder. It is one of the best and most emotional feelings in the world to propose to someone when you have decided to be with that person forever. It's not just a marriage between two people, but a lot more than that.

Before she gets more emotional, Sumrit says pulling up

her chin a bit, 'If you have written the climax in the first one, what have you written in the others?'

'You are so mean,' Adrika says and pokes him on his ribs. He shoves her on the bed and cuddles.

♥

She keeps looking at his eyes as if he has spoken the words she always wanted to hear. He does not answer, but his actions answer on his behalf.

Girls fathom what remains unsaid; they hear what our actions say or eyes convey. They ask questions and wait for the replies. Though they tend not to express their desire for answers, they always wait in sweet anticipation. Adrika lies down on the sofa. Undoubtedly, Sumrit is not going to make it so easy for her.

'You look tired,' he examines, pleasing her on the sofa, which is just big enough to hold both of them.

They understand that having less space is more thrilling. It keeps their desires alive to get more. They entwine themselves into each other and lie on the sofa. The edges push them closer. That is all they need right now.

Adrika is looking at the ceiling, caught in a moment of hesitation to speak or not to speak. Actions speak louder than words. Before she opens her lips, he holds them tightly between his.

His slinks his face down to the folds of her dress. The salty taste of his fingers on the tip of her tongue passes a shiver to her toes. He rolls his finger around her tongue. There is no space for air between the two uncontrolled bodies. Their waists rub with each after. They look like strange statues, the two of them, before they begin to unlock their desires. She looks beautiful. Slim and toned. Calm yet uncontrolled.

The urge is flowing in the dense sea of uncontrolled yearnings and cravings by the two abandoned bodies. She moans, takes a swift breath and lifts her waist. It pains with a jerk but feels divine just at the next moment. It fuels the fire.

His fingers grip her body locking her into his wild wishes. He moves a hand to her neck, and slowly rubbing his tongue on her body, he starts licking the moles on her stomach. He then slides his hand around her thighs, just as they discussed over the phone at times. Those desires are turning into reality one by one. He slides his finger very delicately to the edge of her shoulder, near her collarbone. He begins to take off her shirt with curiosity and care; her perfume still wafting from her innerwear. He wants to own her body. His small acts unite. Even the rough edges of the sofa fuel the fire. The more scratches on their bodies, the more passionate bumps they take. The thrust of the sofa gives them more pleasure, and their passion and intimacy overrules everything around. Their acts run faster than their desires. They take long last breaths before they lose the grip of their fingers. Everything pauses for a while and they go into deep silence.

He rolls down to the floor. Corners of the sofa engulf his shirt and his underpants are lost somewhere behind it. She closes her eyes and stretches her legs in comfort. Happy and satisfied. Rest, she does not want to express.

♥

Dawn is still far away and Adrika does not want to let this moment go without making it memorable for Sumrit. Although Sumrit has not responded to her beautiful way of proposing to him, yet his actions betray his feelings. Adrika concludes that marriage should probably be the next thing to do before she commits any other mistakes in life.

Adrika runs her hand through his hair and goes to pull the curtains aside. She follows the mat on the floor of the hall that leads to the balcony, and basks in the beautiful moonlight view. She looks beautiful, and moonlight on her smooth legs appears so bright. Her beauty gives a new definition of reflection.

Adrika sits in the balcony, resting her chin on her knees and wrapping her hands around her legs. She drifts away in deep thought as she stares back at him on the sofa where he is taking a nap. She rolls her tongue on her lips and smiles. She can smell him on her lips. Dreams take time but reality does not. She wants to see the rest of the things turning into reality before she starts dreaming again. She pauses before imagining things that are yet to happen.

Thinking and smiling, she walks to the small stool placed in the corner of the room where she has kept the bottle of wine she brought for him. His favourite—white wine.

'Sumrit, come! It's nice weather outside.' There is no breeze but she can feel the cold gust on her body.

♥

Sleepy and feeling a bit lethargic, Sumrit follows her to the balcony with a packet of cigarettes.

'I have brought this for you. I hope it's not overrated,' she says, showing him the bottle of wine.

He giggles, 'Not at all.'

They both look far away holding on to the railing.

'Thanks for coming into my life,' Adrika takes a step towards Sumrit and keeps her left hand on his right hand and her chin on his shoulder.

She remembers something that she read somewhere in

Arjun's notebook—only the left and the right hand can hold each other and walk together. That encourages her to ask something she desperately wants to hear.

'You didn't answer my question,' she says, bringing her face in front of his.

'What? I didn't answer? I have come all the way for you,' he smiles and gives her a kiss on her cheeks.

'We have been dating for more than nine months.'

'So are you expecting to have a baby in nine months?' he teases her.

'I am serious. I have told everyone about you. Better be with me, else I will kill you,' she pokes him,

Sumrit moves back. 'Stop it. I will fall down.' He almost hits the bottle of wine.

'Let us finish this before you ruin it all,' he takes it away from her. 'Wait! I will just come,' he goes to the hall and keeps the bottle on the table. He pours a decent amount into two glasses and comes back to the balcony. They sit and have a warm conversation that brings them closer.

It is a universal fact that girls can ask the same question millions of times and you have to answer it a million times. If you don't do so, probably you are breaking the rule of nature and the world may come to an end soon. The question Adrika asks Sumrit remains unanswered.

'I love you and the time we spend together,' says Sumrit, hugging her from behind. It feels good and satisfying.

Adrika relishes the way Sumrit loves her with his words. Intimate conversation is equally effective to make her feel so. He knows it. He is good at it.

They do not realize how the time passes and when they finish the bottle of wine. The night ends up being one of the most memorable nights that they will cherish forever.

Eighteen

EMOTIONS AND MEMORIES do not need time to be felt and recalled. They keep haunting us. It has been more than a month since Adrika moved to Bengaluru and started on her late-night schedules at office. This is not going to be an easy-going job for her—managing a long-distance relationship and the hectic work schedule. She has only heard and read about the term 'work-life balance' in books. Now, she has to use her all analytical and managerial skills to balance it.

Adrika is trying hard to get a relocation, citing that she needs to visit her mother frequently and a move back to Mumbai will be helpful. Everything is fair in love. However, it seems difficult to make everything fair. While her friends are planning for weekends, Adrika is spending her time in office and travel. Moreover, she has to save her leaves so that she can go on a peaceful vacation with Sumrit. Suddenly, in cavernous silence, she feels the vibrations of her cell phone and a flashing message on WhatsApp. It is Ved. The man who always appears digitally or physically, whenever Adrika remembers him. She reads his message.

Someone has forgotten me.

She types.

That would be the last thing in my life.

Adrika becomes happy seeing his message on WhatsApp after

two days. Her fingers running on the touchpad defines her happiness. They run quite fast.

I don't think so.

Why are you talking like that?

I should start hating you.

I have not forgotten you, just busy with work.

How are you?

Ved typing...

21st century girl busy with work.

I am fine.

Well, my mom and sister have come.

They were asking about you.

Ignoring everything that is going on in her life, she feels more excited to know about the arrival of his family. This may help Ved through the tough time in his life. In crisis, we need our family and friends. Moreover, they need us too.

Yeah? That is news.

☺

The happy emoji explains it all. Adrika understands his feelings.

Take them out.

Don't just be busy with your cell phone.

Enjoy your family time, lad.

Tell your busy roommate also ;)

Yes, they are enjoying.

Dimpy Aunty has invited all of us for dinner.

We are just leaving for her place.

Lol. Okay!

All the best.

Dinner at guests' risk.

I am going to miss the fun.

Nobody gets everything :P

Ved teases her but speaks the truth. Adrika is definitely going to miss them. Nothing can replace the time she spent in Mumbai with her friends. It's not just the food we eat at the dinner table, there are emotions, feelings and relationship we make stronger when we talk. That's what she has learnt growing with her father. Now she misses it.

How is Arjun?

Ved checks himself in the washroom mirror and waits for his mother and sister to come out from the room. He takes some time to reply.

He has gone home.

What happened?

Probably, he is trying to be responsible.

True! LOL

No, just joking.

His family has shortlisted one guy for his sister.

So he has gone to meet him.

Ved replies in jest though he is worried about Arjun. They both try to help each other but Arjun is going through a tough time in personal and family life. Both of them can only console each other that everything will be fine with time. Arjun and his family are busy planning a perfect wedding for the only daughter in their family. Indian marriages are not easy, especially arranged marriages. There are a hell lot of expectations. It is like reading a book without its cover page and you do not know anything about it. Whether you will end up reading a good story, a bad story, or a horrific one, nobody really knows.

Arjun is not only worried about his sister but for his own

future also. Someday, what if he tells his mother that he likes Anushka. Moreover, what if they reject her? A family melodrama is to be expected at his home then.

When are aunty and your sister going back?

Most probably in a week.

Oh! I will miss meeting them.

Well, enjoy and have a good family time.

I will ping you later.

Take care!

You too.

Adrika switches her fingers over to the call log, where Arjun is always on the top. She dials his number the next moment.

♥

With a glass of milk and a slice of bread in front of him on the table, Arjun is in deep thoughts. He tries to be realistic about the future challenges he and his family are going to face during his sister's marriage. He knows that he cannot play a big role, taking up the big decisions because the elders have already taken them. However, he is definitely going to be an emotional support for them. Sometimes that is more than enough, when it comes to big occasions. His sister's wedding is the first big event in the family and nobody wants to take any risks—from cheques of lakhs to their honeymoon package, everything has been planned in detail.

Whenever Arjun comes home, his father never shows his happiness, but secretly always wishes to see his son happy and smiling. Probably his ancestors built up that culture to show a heightened sense of respect to one's parents. Arjun has never hugged his father in his whole life.

Seriously!

They both hesitate to show their love for each other. However, this is where inheritance leaves a bad impact on both of them. Sometimes, showing affection is important. They both believe so, but neither does anything about it. His father has always been his idol since childhood, when he used to tell Arjun small incidents of his life. Arjun has seen him working hard and handling life decisions with practicality. Arjun wishes that this outlandish gap in their relationship would go away someday. It has been twenty-six years now!

'Who was on the call?' Arjun's mother asks him. She keeps an eye on everything he does and follows him to every corner he goes to in the big house. A typical suspicious Indian mother.

'Adrika was on the call. She has moved to Bengaluru with a good salary hike,' Arjun says offhandedly. He forgets to tell her that officials have recognized her talent during her training period. Adrika deserves that. She has upgraded her skills over a period.

'I know,' she replies.

Arjun suspects that she must doubt him as he remembers she had a long discussion with Ved over a call last week that Ved wanted to avoid with her, he had ended it by saying that it is 'nothing serious'.

When someone says, 'nothing serious', it actually determines the seriousness.

'Is there any problem? If you will not discuss, how I will come to know?' she asks him.

She knows how to handle him. However, sometimes she becomes too persistent. Perhaps, she has become overprotective of him. Arjun hesitates in discussing his feelings. He always shows his happy and funny side that people love about him. But he has a lot to say.

'There is no problem,' Arjun says. He is just trying to avoid a discussion. Discussing things with someone we trust may not solve the problem, but it definitely gives us courage and belief to face it. That is all we need—courage and belief.

Arjun needs to understand that before he becomes lonelier. Ved has observed him and noticed that he has become quieter in the last few weeks. He has become socially inept. There is something which he is not discussing with him. They even had arguments over this and finally Ved stopped asking him. We lose most relationships because we avoid taking the very small steps of initiation, showing love and affection. Ego wins but in reality, we lose.

She repeats making a guess, 'What are you hiding, Arjun?'

'Nothing,' he says bluntly and she listens calmly.

He continues, 'Mom, please! I am fine. We can discuss this later and I will do as you say. As of now, we should concentrate on the wedding.'

He really does not like discussing things that may disturb him later.

'There is no point talking about these things, Mom. Let's drop it,' he smiles and leaves the lobby where everyone gathers most of the time.

'What are those things?' she asks.

Few wrinkles appear on her forehead and there's doubt in her words. Arjun and his mom share a good bond. However, she has become more possessive about him because she suspects that Dimpy Aunty is eating up all his time, brainwashing and distracting him from the productive things that he does. Well, it's good for him, someone is there to keep an eye on him.

However, Dimpy Aunty has given him brilliant ideas on writing and other important aspects of life, which has changed his personality from a mamma's boy to an independent, responsible man.

Truly, his mother's concern is more concentrated on this change in him rather than knowing anything else. She wants to know if there is anyone else who is taking her son away from her. Either a girl or Dimpy Aunty.

'You are being so independent and have changed so much that you do not need your mother to discuss things, Arjun,' she says what Ved has been saying for the last few weeks. Arjun keeps his empty glass of milk on the slab and turns to her, giving her full attention.

'Probably…' he goes out of his room. She follows him.

'I am talking to you. You can discuss with me, can't you?' she stands in front of him, in doubt and with wrinkles of worry on her forehead.

'You should tell me if I can help you,' she says.

Arjun almost shouts in helplessness in return. The biggest sadness in life is hurting your mother and then regretting it a moment later. Arjun is facing the same plight. He has discussed everything with her, even the first glass of wine he held in his hand. However, for the few ridiculous mistakes he made, she slapped him too. Well, he has been in that tradition of sharing things with her. Thus, it creates an uproar in her mind when Arjun does not share the reason for being so quiet and dejected.

'Let it go, it's nothing!'

'No, you have to tell me.'

'What do you want to know? What do you really want to know?' words tumble out of his mouth. Probably this is the right time to speak out what he feels. Else, hiding his anxiety might lead him into depression once again.

'I want to know what is going on in your mind. You may

feel that I am being overbearing or annoying, but it's okay. That really does not matter to me. You have to tell me.'

♥

Arjun cannot hold his feelings for long. He bursts out in a low emotional voice, 'I have been on medication for a month now. Yes, I have changed because I feel depressed. I have been away from home for years. I get up, go to work and come back. And this monotony just keeps repeating. You were asking me why I stayed at my friends' place. It's because I hate coming back to my place. That silence for hours and hours infests my mind with negative thoughts and I have started feeling that I am good for nothing. I have become fake. I am not able to live like this. I just smile, because others want me to smile. That is frustrating. Really frustrating. But I do.

'I can only pretend to be happy in front of people, but I am really not! I feel very lonely. I am afraid of losing important things in life. That is the reason I take pills. I wasn't telling you because you will be more worried about me. Everything around me is just going wrong. I have not really changed but I am scared of being so,' he feels darkness enveloping him. Arjun turns to the other side and finds his father standing in front of him.

'Who said you are alone?'

Arjun sniffs. His father wraps him in his arms tightly in a hug. The comfort and peace that he waited for years. Arjun needed this so badly. This will help him come out from this depressing phase. The peculiar gap in their relationship has just faded away with an earnest hug. Although a little dramatic, it is worth it for both of them.

'There is no need to go back if you don't feel like. Get well first and spend a good time here before you leave.' Arjun tightens the grip of his fingers on his father's shoulder. That defines his love for his idol. A relationship between a father and a son.

'I haven't hugged you ever. That does not mean I don't care for you. Never think that you are alone…hmm.'

The last word and the way his father keeps his hand on Arjun's head brings more tears into Arjun's eyes. This word has love, care and concern. It makes him stronger. His cheeks are stained with the endless stream of tears. He closes his eyes tightly and chokes with emotion. His father touches his chin, pulls it up a bit, and looks into his moist eyes. His mom feels the happiness by looking at them. His father pats his back softly to encourage him.

'I don't know. I feel so alone and the negativity distracts me over and over again,' Ajrun bursts out into uncontrolled tears.

'It's okay. I will not say that things will be fine like your mom does,' he looks at his mother and smiles.

She knows that he too is emotional but also knows him very well to believe that he will always encourage Arjun to be stronger.

He continues, 'I will just say that…many times we feel that things are not working out and we just keep thinking about it repeatedly because we think we are all alone. In fact, even if there are problems around, they don't need the attention that we give them. That is why we make friends, probably new friends, go on vacation and visit new places. Change is something that everyone needs. In relationships, in work and the way we live our life. We live in the 21st century and in the 21st century, men also cry. So, it's okay. If you want to react to something, you should react but never keep them in your heart.'

He smiles looking at Arjun, who wipes his tears and hides his face in his hands. Arjun does feel comfortable after this conversation which is followed by a warm hug.

They all sit at the table for breakfast.

Nineteen

NOT EVERY EVENING can be so pampering for Arjun. Therefore, he has become conscious and does not speak for a while—nothing about Adrika or about his own problems. Arjun guesses that she was on call with someone a few minutes before. Relatives play a big role in ruining your life.

'Arjun, where were you last Saturday?' his mom asks him at the dining table, suspiciously breaking the father-son conversation that left the mother out.

It is 6.30 p.m. This is the time when all common conversations happen at the table. However, Arjun had his personal conversation with her sometime back—sitting on the kitchen slab while she was making tea and snacks. She did not ask him where he was last Saturday then.

'I was in Mumbai,' being a little conscious, he replies.

'That I know. You live in Mumbai but where in Mumbai? Why didn't you pick my call then?' she asks in the same breath. Arjun understands what she is trying to know.

'I was at Anushka's home,' he says and gets ready to answer all the questions she is going to ask.

'Weekends are for rest and you roam around. What about your book? Are you being an irresponsible author?' the tone of her voice made her words sound harsher.

She is not at all concerned about him writing a book, because she knows Arjun will do that on time. Her only intention is to keep him away from Anushka's mother, probably. There are two ways to stop someone from doing particular things. His mother does it by not saying things in a straightforward manner. She becomes uncomfortable when Arjun interrupts her in the middle of a conversation. No matter what respect and pride he carries for her, sometimes it is better to remain silent in front of her.

'I am asking something. I know these Mumbai people. They don't know our culture. Your dad and I have spent all our lives trying to make things better for you and your sister. Don't get trapped in anything. Girls are very smart these days. We will find a good Brahmin girl for you,' she says as if she has travelled across the country.

'So you think finding a so-called good girl is easy? Well, you have visited Mumbai twice. You should not judge anyone without meeting. You say so yourself, don't you?' Arjun speaks up courageously.

'Now you are defending her? Probably I have said that in some other reference. Moreover, there are good girls; I have shortlisted a few for you.'

'Why would I defend her? Shortlisted? Like a materialistic thing?' he asks his in sarcasm.

'Yes the perfect one for you. Or do you like her?' she questions him.

'Probably yes,' he says casually.

'If you are not sure, you should concentrate on your life,' she opens her box of suggestions as if she is just one move away from checkmate.

'I am sure. I just said 'probably' because my surety should not be a cause of your disappointment.'

'So this is one of your worries?' she asks. His dad looks at him. He has kept quiet through the last few minutes. He does not want to interfere a mother-son discussion. He knows that you should speak only when you know that your words will be taken into consideration. He gets up and goes into the other room, picking up the last potato chip.

'No, not at all.'

Arjun *must* have some secrets. He is the son of a suspicious mother.

♥

'You are being so mischievous these days. You do not pick my calls. You don't discuss things with me anymore and…' she says, putting effort into her words to make Arjun understand that she also expects things from him.

'And what…?' Arjun wants to know what else she knew about him.

'You should not talk to Adrika,' she says in a straightforward manner. Without expecting any reply from Arjun, she continues, 'We are concentrating on your sister's wedding. I do not want you to create any issues. You know how difficult and sensitive these relations are.'

'But what happened?' Arjun asks in surprise.

'Why are you being so helpful to Adrika? There is no need to call her from now. I do not like such attachments which may question you and your family,' she becomes harsh and says things that Arjun did not expect from her.

'But what happened?' he repeats in frustration.

All mothers are eligible for Ekta Kapoor's daily soaps. They create so much irrelevant suspense. Arjun knows very well that nobody can brainwash her, but he also suspects that something is brewing.

Arjun asks, 'Why do you think so?'

He adds, 'She is my cousin, even more than a cousin. She has helped me in my worst days when nobody did. Nobody.

I know there are family differences, but we do not have any differences between us. Moreover, people will always gossip for no reason. They have been gossiping from the day she lost her father. They have been gossiping from the day her relationship became the topic of discussion among all relatives without even thinking what situation she was going through at that time. Why are we putting so much pressure on her?'

She interrupts, 'It's not just about talking or guiding her. You have helped her. She is settled. Now you focus on your career and life.'

'No, she does not need spoon-feeding. Moreover, she has all the right that anybody else does.'

'Arjun you are taking me wrong, completely,' she wants to explain her side of things, that there are a few questions being raised about her character from the moment the family got to know about her relationship.

We talk about rights and equality and then we forget everything about them when it comes to reality.

It's her personal decision what she wants to do with her life, but our own people do not understand it. Somewhere, they will equally blame Arjun because he has forgotten the family culture he has grown up into. When relatives who considered themselves modern started suggesting to her father that Adrika should do a Bachelor of Arts and then probably get married as the other girls did in the family, it was Arjun who talked to her father to encourage her to enrol herself in the same college he was doing his engineering from.

Arjun gets up and asks her directly, 'What happened? Did someone say anything about her? Did Ved call you?' Arjun starts asking questions.

'You do not know what has happened? What the relatives are talking about?' she questions back.

'I know them well.'

'She is living with someone out of marriage.'

Her words shock him.

'What?' Arjun does not believe her. 'Who told you?'

'You really do not know?' she asks again.

'No, I do not know that she is in a live-in relationship,' Arjun is trying hard to connect all the dots, but fails to make a clear picture. He still does not believe but does not doubt his mother too.

'You know what it will do to our and her reputation in the society? Do you even have an idea of what would happen if someone comes to know about this? Will the boy really get married to your sister? Think, your sister is a professor with Masters in computer science. Even then it has been difficult for us to find a guy for her even after giving so much dowry unwillingly.'

'That's what I hate about them,' says Arjun.

Arjun is about to speak in clarification but pauses.

'She lives in Bengaluru and this is the first time I heard about all this.'

'Your uncle's son lives in Bengaluru. He told me about her,' she says.

'I do not know how he knows. However, you do not tell this to anybody, I'll talk to Adrika casually. Mom! Do not stress. I know her. Do not just go with what others say. I will ask her if it's true. And you should stop talking to people about this stuff,' Arjun tells her.

♥

No matter how strong we keep the bond with our friends, but at times a relationship of love surrenders. Adrika used to fight with Arjun and Ved for not giving her time. Now that anger has vanished somewhere. Probably, a new growing relationship has taken their place in the busy schedule of her life.

Though Adrika messaged Ved and Arjun about her arrival in Mumbai the previous day, Ved was occupied with his work and Arjun was not in town. He has become busier these days. Ved and Arjun had an argument last week, Ved believed that Arjun should give his friends some time, at least his roommate, rather than working all the time. Yet, after complaining to Dimpy Aunty, Arjun has again started writing and cooking.

However, Arjun is improving over the last few months. Cooking works for him as a stress buster. It maybe unbelievable but he has received a note of five hundred rupees in shagun from Dimpy Aunty, and that too for cooking at her home. Everyone liked the food and Anushka's father, who is always judgemental about everything, had actually made a clean swipe of his plate. Arjun will be a great future partner. These creatures are rare around us. Anushka should really think before saying no to him if he proposes to her someday.

♥

Leaving her mind in Bengaluru, taking her heart with her, Adrika proceeds to Mumbai. Finally, the day Adrika and Sumrit are to meet has arrived. Adrika passes the beautiful valleys of the Bengaluru-Mumbai highway. The moment she enters the bus, she remembers Arjun as her eyes fall on what was written on top of the first row of seats—only for pregnant women. Arjun always prefers that seat because of its comfort. He does not like travelling in buses unless they are luxury ones.

She looks around and prefers to take the same seat. She'll give it up if anyone in need turns up.

A relationship changes us in all ways. Actually, it is a matter of time and the people we give priority to. The girl, who was afraid of travelling in buses, is now going to enjoy the solo trip to Mumbai. Adrika settles down with her earphones and a long playlist of romantic songs, which are Sumrit's favourites too.

She closes her eyes. Engrossed in the long list of songs, as time travels with the wheels, she forgets to pick up a few calls from Arjun.

Twenty

IT WILL TAKE ages to understand the obsession girls have with the sea and waves. Do boys also have that fascination with the seaside and the open sky? Or are all their fantasies limited to places with a roof? But to think of it, a lot can happen under the roof...

Adrika plans to ask him to meet her at the seaside. No matter how many times you meet someone, every time it feels so different when you are in love. Every meeting feels more exciting than the previous one. That is the beauty of it. Sometimes it floats. Sometimes it runs deep.

Carrying her handbag on her shoulder with a sleepy face, she decides to sit at a restaurant, which has been one of her preferred places to freshen up due to its clean changing room and washrooms. She will definitely use the time to get ready in the smallest washroom while the waiter brings her iced tea. Management is the mother of all skills. She is probably the grandmother of them.

She appears in a black dress that looks stunning on her toned body. It fits her sculpted body, and she has teamed it up with a scarf. A relationship changes a person in all ways. Physical appearance is one of them. Adrika has become prettier over time.

It is always a little colder at the seaside. Therefore, she carries a jacket on her shoulder that covers half of the tattoo on her neck. She had got it done along with Sumrit in Bengaluru when they met the last time. Small acts of craziness.

Even if it was normal weather, she would have done the same. There are girls who feel comfortable and confident carrying one extra piece of clothing on their bodies. She is one of them. Few people stare at her. She reaches her table, takes some time to finish her iced tea, and leaves before she gets late. She knows that Sumrit never reaches on time, so she has called him an hour before.

♥

The aroma of coffee from the nearest coffee shop mingles in the air. Adrika enjoys this transitory moment of anticipation. It is worth waiting out here.

With the intense sea on one side and the dazzling Bandstand on the other, it is the idyllic place for a romantic young couple. She stops a couple of times along the way to take in the beautiful views of the skyline, the sea, the beach, couples and herself, restricting herself from doing crazy things that she used to do with Iona.

She pauses for a moment and her mind goes back to the discussion she had with Ved. Soon, she will forget the bond she used to share with Iona. People change with time.

She buys a water bottle from a hawker, sits on the sidewalk and with eager eyes waits for Sumrit.

Adrika is checking her face on the phone's screen when she spots Sumrit standing and looking around, and then concentrates on his phone. Probably trying to call her.

She stares at him for a moment before approaching him. She is not just checking out his back but the man she loves. She has the right to.

Sumrit is wearing a white shirt and blue jeans; a few drops

of sweat are trickling down his neck. He has a well-built figure; all athletes have the same physique—broad shoulders and a wide chest. He is not just looking handsome and cool, but stunning.

Although, generally girls are tagged with the word 'hot' for their beauty, yet today he deserves it completely for his handsomeness. Adrika walks towards him to surprise him as she has reached an hour before him.

'This is not done,' Adrika says calmly standing behind him. He turns back with a broad smile to greet her.

'You will never understand how it feels to wait for someone and that too with no apologies,' she says. It embarrasses him.

'I am sorry. I got late.'

He is eager to add more, 'We had a football match.'

'Congratulations. Hope you didn't lose that.'

'Unfortunately, we did.'

They settle down at a roadside café.

♥

Adrika wants to avoid this place but Sumrit has already planned to go the café. She needs a quiet place this time as she has a few things to discuss. She is looking forward to taking this relationship ahead.

They enter and get comfortable in one corner of the café. A place for four it is. She smiles remembering something. We all have an emotional core no matter how strong we are. We do cry for someone we love. Before Adrika manages to order something, the waiter serves them a dish of large golden brown potato shells, fried and filled with Jack and Cheddar cheese along with crisp seasoned bacon and green onions.

'Quite impressive,' Adrika raises her eyebrows in appreciation. Sumrit has planned everything perfectly. He has improved a lot since their last argument.

'Thanks,' he bends his head down in response. Adrika smirks and takes a small sip of his drink.

The music gets louder. Sumit claps on the table in excitement. The smoke in the café swirls around. She rolls the ice cube in the glass.

Her phone rings. It is Ajrun. She walks to the corner of the cafe from where she can see Sumrit diagonally, and takes the call.

'Hello, how are you?' she asks.

'I am good. Have you reached Mumbai?' Arjun asks.

'Yes, today. When are you coming back? You have become so much busier. You don't even reply to my messages,' she says looking at Sumrit stepping towards the smoking zone.

Sumrit waves and calls her to the smoking zone.

'I have just reached today,' Arjun says and continues, 'when are we meeting?'

'I am always ready and you are always busy. We need to figure out a time,' she articulates and walks to the smoking zone. Sumrit digs into his pocket for a minute before dragging out a cigarette. Adrika raises an eyebrow as he lights it and takes a drag before blowing out a puff of smoke.

'Did you tell anything to Ved or anybody about Sumrit?' he asks abruptly.

'What happened?'

'You did not tell me that you were staying with Sumrit in Bengaluru.'

Arjun must have thought that he will meet her and discuss this, but he cannot control himself from asking and clearing out things.

The one who asks him before doing any damn little thing has taken the decision of living together with someone.

'I want to meet you Arjun,' Adrika utters being aware and

a little startled by his words.

'Someone has told me, and you know how Aunty will feel if she comes to know about it…'

Sumrit was doing a month-long internship in Bengaluru. It had all started with frequent visits, which turned into overnight stays. They did not mind and ended up staying together. Sumrit stayed over at her place while Adrika's flatmate, one of her colleagues, was out of the country for a month.

There is a completely different life behind clothes and glossy faces, and it is necessary to know everything about the person you decide to be with the rest of your life. Being a 21st century, self-dependent girl, Adrika understands that a relationship is not just about sex. It actually starts after that part is over. They did have arguments, but Adrika has always given her best to make this relationship happier and deeper.

Everyone wants to speak about gender equality but in reality, they want girls to cook, to raise kids, and to take care of a family because they think it is only their duty to do so, even when girls work equally hard at the workplace. And the girls still do all of it because they are deeply in love.

'Arjun, I will tell you in detail once we meet,' Adrika responds in a hurry.

'Okay.' Arjun disconnects the call.

Adrika feels a void within for a moment. Maybe it is because of the way Arjun disconnected the phone call. She goes to where Sumrit is anxiously sucking in the velvet smoke. He releases a cloud of smoke on her face as she draws near.

'When are you quitting this?' she says through gritted teeth and crosses her arms. Adrika hates it when he smokes.

'You need to stop smoking before I start hating you,' she gives him a soft punch on his ribs.

'Hmm...hmm,' Sumrit comes closer trying to kiss her. There

is no one in the tiny smoking zone. Adrika suddenly feels the coldness on her lips.

'Stop it. Someone will see us,' Adrika holds his hands before he comes closer.

Adrika takes a step back. She feels dizzy and unwell. The next moment she runs towards the washroom. Sumrit flicks the cigarette butt into the bin and follows her.

♥

Adrika washes her face with some cold water and feels better. On her way back to the table, several questions arise in her mind. She realizes they may disturb her if she does not ask Sumrit what she intends to. She has been thinking about asking Sumrit when he plans to talk to his family about her, so that she can tell her mother about him.

'What happened?' Sumrit asks, with apparent signs of worry on his face.

'Nothing, I have been travelling since last night…so probably…dizziness. Buses are my enemies. I am fine,' Adrika tries to make him comfortable with an artificial grin. She wipes her face and drinks a glass of water. She gathers some courage and speaks to Sumrit.

'Arjun had called…'

'What was he saying?' Sumrit asks.

'Nothing, just casual talk.' Adrika pauses.

In a relationship, when words seem less effective in describing feelings and emotions, then the relationship requires more attention and extra care.

'So you haven't answered yet,' says Adrika affectionately. Adrika becomes a little worried while asking.

'What?' he asks.

'Don't get me wrong, but my friends and a few family members know about you.'

He smiles, 'So you have been discussing us with Arjun.'

'Yes, he is my cousin and he cares for me,' Adrika says gravely.

Words are more powerful than emotions because they initiate feelings. Adrika does not want to take the risk of making this conversation difficult for both of them. She only wants to know the status of this relationship—where it is headed to. She does not want to get hurt once more. Silence is making her patience stale.

Adrika continues after a pause, 'I am not forcing you to do anything. I know you have other priorities, so do I. But we can at least talk about it to our families. Once families are involved, we can both take our time.'

'So that means you do not trust me?' Sumrit asks her brusquely. He takes a sip of water.

'I do not mean it. It is not about getting worried or not trusting you. If I did not trust you, I would not have stayed with you for a month, sharing the same bed. I am sure that you love me too.'

'Of course I love you,' says Sumrit.

'Yes, I love you too. You have touched each part of my body. I slept with you because I was sure about you. This relationship means everything to me. It is not infatuation or lust,' Adrika shows him a few marks on her hands which she got when he hit her during an argument a month before. He hides them with his hand without a word.

'First love was emotional but this is a mature decision I have taken. Do not leave me half way. I already have a bad past. That scares me sometimes,' her words show that emotions often become a weakness when it comes to a relationship.

Though she is an independent girl, she is emotional at heart. Love has been both her strength and weakness.

'Everything will be fine. Adrika, do not get me wrong. I do not mean to hurt you. I just need some time. And I have apologized for the mistakes I have made in this relationship.'

Everyone has a past, what if it becomes an intimidating baggage and tumbles over into the future? Adrika is sure about Sumrit and knows his answer, but she gets afraid because of her past. She relates everything that's going on in her life with what had happened in the past. Our past teaches us not to make the same mistakes in the future.

The waiter keeps the bill on the table before Adrika finishes the glass of water.

'Wait, I'll pay,' Adrika smiles.

Sumrit smiles back.

'Chill! It does not affect your manhood,' she blinks.

'But definitely male empowerment,' Sumrit laughs.

Adrika pays the bill and they walk to the exit with a few unanswered questions. Adrika skips the plan to meet Ved and Arjun. She hopes that Arjun will not mind. She can meet him if she wants to, but she does not have answers to the questions Arjun may ask her...not yet.

Next day they spend some alone time at Surmit's place and then she leaves for Bengaluru.

Twenty-one

IT IS EARLY morning, when the heavy rain has reduced to a drizzle. Therefore, Adrika sleeps again after snoozing the alarm for ten minutes. Those ten minutes turn into half an hour that she does not realize.

She slept late the previous night, holding her cell phone in her hand and trying to reach Sumrit, who was unreachable.

The sun rises a little up in the sky when the hands of the tableside clock reach 7.20. Slowly opening an eye, she looks at the wall clock. She gets up as if someone has punched her. She is already late for work, when her cell phone beeps an arrival of a WhatsApp message. She jumps on the bed and grabs her phone, as if she is fighting with her bed for it. Think of her man, and he is virtually here. It is Sumrit. Probably apologizing for his disappearance last night.

Adrika opens the message in anticipation.

Hi Adrika,

Please read this with patience. I know it is cowardly of me to ping you on WhatsApp rather than calling or telling you directly when you asked me that we should talk to our families. Adrika, I know we had many fights in the last few months that nobody knows of. Everyone just sees the smiles that we both present.

You are the kind of girl that any guy will want in his life, but I want to say something that I have felt over the last few months with you. You loved me truly and I always tried to love you back. I was always attracted to both your innocence and intelligence. You have inspired me. I enjoyed every moment we spent together in those 30 days we lived together, even those days when you came to meet me in Mumbai. I believe that you felt the same.

Adrika, I like you a lot and I want you to be happy. Please get it out of your mind that I ever thought of leaving you.

Why would I have?

We loved each other so much and there was no reason to leave. A girl who took care of everything in my life, why would I leave her?

It is a dream of every guy to be with someone like you.

Adrika, you are the one who makde me feel strong when I was feeling low. It makes me smile when I recall those stupid little things we did.

However, I wanted to share many things with you, Adrika. I know I am the reason of all the fights. I have done things which I should never have. Hope you forgive me. However, this is true that I loved you a lot more than I loved anyone else in my life.

But, whenever I changed myself for our love, it couldn't match to your feelings. Eventually, I stopped doing anything for our relationship. I wanted to share many things with you but every time we fought, we just ended up getting physically intimate. The nights we spent together left me deeply unhappy because I hurt you by shouting at you and disrespecting you.

I know you will not forgive me for this, but our relationship is just an infatuation that I feel. What if we cannot find happiness even after years of being together?

I do not blame you in any manner, but consider myself the culprit. I did try my best to keep loving you, but failed. I don't feel the same that I used to when we met for the first time.

I respect that you have changed a lot for me. However, we cannot be with each other because I cannot play with your feelings. I know it is tough for you, but please know that it's not easy for me either. I am going home today because I cannot be here like this.

Hope you forgive me.

Once that first tear breaks free, the rest follow in an unbroken stream. Standing near her bed, her legs start shaking.

She does not even know how to react to this. She wipes her tears and calls Sumrit.

♥

We become so weak when love becomes our weakness. The girl who has never surrendered to any tough situation in life, finds everything around her gloomy in just a few moments. Everything seems worthless without Sumrit. Her eyes fill with tears again, one slow tear slips out, rolling down her cheek. She tries to wipe it away as quickly as possible. She tries to wrap her mind around why this is happening to her all over again. She has come back to the same place where she was years before. She is helpless and heartbroken in love, once again.

Adrika redials Sumrit's number but he is still not reachable. Her lips quake as she feels a coldness take over her body. She controls her tears and stops herself from crying. She just gulps down her anxiety.

Though disheartened, she courageously takes her backpack out of the cupboard and throws the things out of it in the corner of the bed. She puts some clothes and some sanitary pads into the bag. Life is not always what we imagine or dream of it; it just takes a moment or a blink to change it. That has happened to Adrika.

Adrika boards the bus from Bengaluru to Mumbai. The routes are the same but some journeys make us smile, while some make us cry. It does not matter what seat she gets today and she does not need any song to give her company. With wet eyes and a dry throat, she waits to reach Mumbai as soon as possible.

She starts typing a WhatsApp message.

Sumrit, it is not compulsory that you cannot fall in love with someone else. That is as natural as the way you fell in love with me. You can feel exactly the same, or even better than what you felt with me. However, this is temporary. You will be in the same situation years later. Then you will realize 'it was like an illusion', but then it will be too late for us.

So, if you are thinking 'am I with the right person?' or 'am I the right person to be loved', please get rid of such thoughts. You should understand that I changed myself just for this relationship and never spoke about it because I wanted it to grow stronger.

A successful and lifelong relationship is not about finding the right person or feeling the same way as we used to. It's about learning to love the person we have in our life. It is not so easy, but we both have to work on it. I am always there for you. Please just meet me once. I am coming to Mumbai.

♥

It is written in ancient books that sharing grief with people reduces the pain we go through. In reality, it is rare to find people who lessen our pain.

'Is everything alright?' an old man sitting next to her in the bus asks, looking doubtfully at her.

You do not share all your problems with just anyone. Therefore, she says with a phony smile, 'Yes. I am fine.'

Nervously, she tries to adjust herself and impatiently waits for these few hours to pass.

Adrika starts feeling ill and depressed. She would have taken the train if it wasn't for her irregular menstruation that was troubling her for the last couple of months. She blames it on the glitches in her work and the situation she is going through in her personal life.

She still has a few hours to reach Mumbai.

She feels as if she cannot not face it. She wants to hide

herself under her stole. When problems come, they come from all sides. The painful time she is going through, cannot really be explained in words. She squeezes herself and closes her eyes. She ignores everything happening around her. She just wants to reach Mumbai. She wants to meet Sumrit.

♥

Uncomfortable and grouchy, she comes out of the public lavatory at the bus stop. The giant clock hanging under the shed at the bus stop displays 10.45 p.m.

She thinks of calling Ved, but the situation demands her to call either Sumrit or Arjun at this time.

She stops. She does not want to tell Arjun about it.

She ignores all the nonsensical ideas and dials the number of one of her friends, Neha, who was her roommate for a few weeks in Mumbai. She is not reachable. This reminds her of Sumrit. She thinks of calling him, but nothing has changed overnight.

Her shivering fingers call Neha's mother. These rings take time to pass before she picks up the call.

'Hi Aunty, this is Adrika, Neha's friend. May I talk to her?' She asks Neha's mother and calculates the time she will require to reach their place from the bus stop.

'Hi beta! Neha has gone to Goa with her friends. You can call on her number,' she replies.

Adrika hears a few beeps of call waiting on her phone. She guesses it's her mother as she missed her a couple of calls from last night.

'Okay, Aunty I will call her. Thank you,' saying so Adrika disconnects the call.

♥

This is how we change priorities in life; there was a time when Adrika and her mother used to talk for hours without worrying about time, phone bills or anything else.

'Where are you, Adrika? I have been trying your number since yesterday,' her worried mother asks.

Adrika senses the distress in her words.

Adrika wants to disconnect the call saying that she is fine before her mother asks her more questions. Adrika walks behind the ticket counter, far away from the bus lobby, to avoid the uproar.

She articulates, 'I am at office, had some urgent work. I will leave in sometime. I'll call you once I reach home.'

This is how circumstances change us. Today, she has lied to her mother. Tears of guilt run down her cheeks.

'I was trying your number for the last few hours,' her mother says.

Adrika interrupts, 'I will call you once I reach home.'

'Okay! Take care and have something before you leave. Avoid eating late at night, it is already too late,' her mother says.

Adrika hangs up the call saying, 'Okay'.

She realizes her biggest mistake was falling in love.

She walks fast to the exit while scrolling down the long list of contacts. She accepts the reality that no one can really help her when she needs it the most.

Any relationship needs our effort to make it stronger, which she has failed to give in her relationships with her friends or family. She has become weaker by being away from them.

She had put all her efforts in her relationship with Sumrit. She feels even more helpless. All these bitter thoughts make her ask herself why she tries to be in a relationship when she has already lost everything. Before she gets weaker, she follows her instinct not to call Arjun. She calls Anushka without giving it any thought. She may not be able to explain everything to Arjun and will end up crying.

She hopes that Anushka will understand her situation.

Twenty-two

LYING IN BED next to Anushka since midnight, Adrika keeps trying Sumrit's number.

It is 6.05 a.m. when the alarm starts beeping on her phone again. She had snoozed it thrice since 5.30, which is her jogging time.

Anushka tries to wake Adrika up but she pretends that she is unwell and wants to sleep some more. Anushka lets her sleep. Adrika has not told her yet why she has suddenly arrived at her place.

Adrika feels the darkness around her will soon swallow her. Lying with her head buried in her hands, she rocks back and forth, sobbing inconsolably. She wraps her arms tightly around herself. Her pillow is wet and her cheeks are stained with the endless stream of tears. She hides her face before Anushka notices, and trying to comfort herself, she puts her head on her knees. She closes her eyes tightly and feels as if she is choking.

'Is everything okay?' Anushka asks her.

There is no reply to her question except a few sniffs. Anushka understands in a moment that there is something wrong.

'Hey, what happened?' she asks again. She holds her shoulder, pulls her a bit closer and looks into her bloodshot eyes. Anushka hugs her, and those little sniffs turns into a big cry.

'What happened? You are the strongest girl I have ever met. Trust me! I mean it. Do not cry like this. Tell me what happened,' she asks patting Adrika on the back. That may give her some encouragement. But she fails.

Adrika has been good to everyone. She has become everyone's favourite in a short time.

Love does not see the physical or mental strength, it makes you weak and turns your life upside down. Adrika bursts out uncontrollably.

Without asking anything more, Anushka hugs her tightly and lets the tears come out. She keeps patting her on her shoulder and runs one hand on her head until she stops crying.

The clock is still moving like a snail. It says 6.15 a.m. when they hear clacking of footsteps in the hall. It must be Dimpy Aunty starting her day, doing basic household stuff.

Adrika releases herself from the hug and looks around, wiping her face.

Before Dimpy Aunty asks a number of questions to both of them, Anushka gets up and shuts the door to the room. She takes Adrika to the sofa and opens the window to let the cool morning breeze come in. Adrika needs fresh air.

Anushka is her only source of courage and support when she feels completely shattered. The heart does not know its age, it cries when it breaks. When someone hurts, you cry. This is when we realize that we are humans.

Sitting on the sofa with Anushka, Adrika tells her everything, starting from the first day when she met Sumrit. Her throat is dry and she is still feeling dizzy and weak. She has a problem travelling in buses. Moreover, she has travelled during her period.

♥

We forget all ethics or etiquettes when it comes to saving a relationship. Tired and dejected, Adrika still keeps trying to call Sumrit.

After long strings of passing rings, Sumrit picks up the phone.

Almost as if she has a new life now, she says, 'Why were you not picking my call? Where are you?'

'Adrika, I am on the way to my hometown. Please stop calling me. It's not easy for me also but there is no point hurting each other,' Sumrit says with no emotions in his words.

Dimpy Aunty enters while she is on the call, standing in the balcony.

'When did she come?' she asks Anushka, looking at her in doubt.

'Do not look at me like I am a thief,' she grins at her and continues, 'You were sleeping when she came. So I did not want to wake you up.'

'Who is she talking to?' she asks, her second major question.

However, she has already squeezed in several micro questions in between.

'I don't know,' Adrika hears Anushka's reply to Dimpy Aunty and then tries to hide her face.

Adrika is stranded and weary. When after some time she cannot bear it, she starts calling him in anger and records angry voice messages on WhatsApp, 'I know you do not want to talk to me but I have come to Mumbai just to meet you. May I come to meet you? Please.'

Even her anger has a sense of pleading. For that moment, she abuses herself as the biggest failure. Dimpy Aunty looks at her once again. She turns her face and pretends as if she is talking to her mother.

She begs him and keeps sending him messages on WhatsApp. All of a sudden, her cell phone rings. It is Sumrit.

'Adrika, what are you doing? I am not in Mumbai; I cannot meet you. You didn't ask me before coming to Mumbai, so go back,' he says in the same tone, same anger. Nothing has changed. If something has changed, it is her face, her feelings. Her body is sweating, face is red, and head is burning. She is in pain. She feels dizzier and weaker.

Anushka announces, 'Hey Adrika, let us have breakfast.'

'Yeah coming,' she tilts her head towards the room to hide her tears. She is regretting her decision to come to Mumbai.

She lied to her mom yesterday and is going to tell a few more lies at the breakfast table. She takes a few steps to the table and touches Dimpy Aunty's feet to greet her.

'Good morning!'

'Good morning,' Dimpy Aunty smiles and adds, 'Is everything fine?'

'Yes, Aunty,' she responds with a phony leer. Suddenly she feels as if there is a tight band around her head. She squeezes her eyes shut. She has been travelling since yesterday.

'Do you need water?' Anushka asks.

'I will just come back in a minute,' she walks towards to the washroom. Her steps do not have strength. She loses control and falls on the sofa before Anushka runs to hold her.

A sudden blackout.

Twenty-three

THE SUN IS pouring in some light through the gaps in the curtains, reminding her of the old memories which are more painful and hurt her every time she tries to come out of her pain. Everything seems gloomy to her. She tries to divert her mind by finding reasons to help herself get through the sadness, but fails repeatedly.

Adrika looks at the little blips that are displayed on the monitor every time with her heartbeat and then she looks at the bottle of glucose held in a stand.

Adrika is suffering from chronic depression. The doctor has said that she has a persistent depressive disorder, dysthymia. Moreover, this has not just happened in a week or a month. She must have been going through this for months or maybe years. The doctor has said that this happens when you repeatedly keep thinking about certain things. Later, when it gets worse, your own thoughts drag you there even if you do not want to remember them. That causes persistent depression.

Anushka does not want to tell Adrika about it. However, Dimpy Aunty tells her, knowing that she has the courage to fight it.

Adrika starts connecting the dots and notices her irregular behaviour, hopelessness, her lack of productivity, the low self-esteem and an overall feeling of inadequacy. She realizes that she cannot sleep at nights even after high doses of sleeping pills. Observations and reports do not lie.

The doctor has suggested Dimpy Aunty to keep her in the hospital for a few days and treat her well in a positive environment. Else, severe depression can lead to a permanent mental disorder. After that, without having further discussion on this, Anushka and Arjun decide to keep her in the hospital.

♥

It is dusk and the lights are dim. Adrika is in bed, curled up within the confines of her brown blanket and controlling her emotions within it. Her emotions are dry as dust and she does not want to share her sentiments with anyone.

Though awake, she does not want to get out of bed. She wonders what is wrong with her life. She feels lonelier when her colleagues or friends come to see her at the hospital. It is difficult to smile when it does not come from the heart.

Only a few people understand you when you go through a tough time in life. The rest just watch and judge you. Yes, they do. That is one of the saddest truths of materialistic relationships. She does not want to meet so many people. What she really wants to do, she does not know. She only wants to meet Sumrit and tell that everything will be fine if they both work on it.

Does everyone go through this phase in life or is it just me who is suffering? She wonders.

She tries to avoid such questions but she wants answers from within. She had lost her father at an early stage of life, then she lost her first love and then again, she has failed in love. Moreover, she has lost the trust of her friends and her mother who always had faith in her. That hurt her the most. Regret is a slow death that kills you every day.

When we run away from things, they seem to haunt us

repeatedly. She can't just forget things that happened to her. She begins thinking about the past. There are so many memories, ones that made her happy. Yet the overpowering memories are the ones associated with negative emotions. She thinks of her present, the frustrations which seem to have gripped her life. She is tense. Her head is aching and burning. Her eyes are red. Still, she tries to control her emotions.

'Am I responsible for all that has happened to me?'

'Will this affect my family and friends?'

'I cannot afford to trouble my mom anymore. I have messed up too many times in the past. I deserve nothing better. I have broken the trust of everyone. I can't live like this.'

Arjun is sitting on the sofa when Adrika hears some clacking on the floor. Before she guesses, she finds Dimpy Aunty and Anushka entering her room.

♥

'How are you?' Dimpy Aunty asks before Arjun recognizes her voice from the back.

'Hi Aunty. I am good,' he gets up out of respect and leaves a place for her to come and sit on the sofa, which is adjacent to the bed. Her appearance itself made everyone smile. We all have a few people who spread positive vibes around. Dimpy Aunty is one of them, though she troubles Arjun a lot when he is around.

Anushka comes a step ahead and gives a smile looking at Adrika. 'Hey, how are you now?' she murmurs.

'Where is Ved?' Dimpy Aunty enquires as if she is investigating something.

'I told him to leave. He will come later,' Arjun replies. Arjun is staying with Adrika tonight; he does not seem well as he has recurring headaches while walking. It is not major but it irritates him. Probably he is taking too much stress. He knows that its cause is his work. However, giving his health second priority, he wants to talk to Adrika. Adrika must have told him to stay as well. It may help to heal her pain with his company.

Dimpy Aunty approaches Adrika. 'How are you now?' she says keeping her hand on her head.

Adrika has become proficient at faking a smile. She pretends to look happy but everything reminds her of her situation, and she fails to give a fake smile.

'Fine,' the only word she speaks.

'Are you okay?' Anushka comes closer and asks.

'Is this is critical stage of hypertension?' Adrika asks her brusquely. She wants to hear that she will be fine. Maybe words don't heal the pain but they matter a lot when we are in pain. The core of her eye moves to Dimpy Aunty in hope to get the answer.

Before Arjun says anything, Anushka says, 'There is nothing critical. You have just lost seven kilograms, but that you have always wanted.'

'How much does she weigh now?' Arjun tries to keep the surrounding positive and happy.

'Probably 55 kg?' Anushka blinks at her.

'You guys are crazy?' Adrika keeps her palm on the bed and tries to feel the texture. That feels cold and good to her. However, her instinct demands a human touch.

'You need to take care of yourself,' Arjun says holding her hand, while Dimpy Aunty sits on the other side of the bed.

'There is nothing to worry about. Just think positive and take care. Everything will be fine,' Dimpy Aunty tells her in her own way.

Probably her presence will make Adrika comfortable.

'Can you guys go out for some time?' the doctor announces entering the room and reaching the bed, as if she is in a hurry.

'Sure,' Arjun says and they go out of the room.

♥

Arjun is still standing at the door, keeping it ajar, listening to the conversation. In the last couple of days, the doctor has become his friend. Arjun is good at conversations.

'You can take Aunty to the cafeteria. You have not had anything since morning,' Arjun tells Anushka before the doctor comes out of the room.

'Yes,' Anushka looks at her mom, 'let's go.'

Anushka comes a step closer to him, 'Are you fine?'

'Yeah,' Arjun says in response.

'Arjun! Either Ved or I will stay tonight. You go home and take rest,' she says.

Dimpy Aunty says, 'Yes! If you are not feeling well, go home. Anushka can stay here tonight. There is no need to be the hero all the time. If you are healthy, only then can you keep others healthy.'

'Okay, you both eat something, we will see,' Arjun says. They walk to the lift to go the cafeteria on the ground floor.

Arjun takes a few steps back smiling at the doctor while she exits.

♥

Arjun enters the room, sits on the left side of the bed, and places his hand on her forehead.

'What are you doing, Arjun?' Adrika says, being uncomfortable. He still remembers that she used to oil his head when they were home during summer vacations.

She feels a little awkward. Maybe she feels guilty over what she has done and how she has troubled him.

'Why are you crying?' Arjun asks her and makes himself strong not to cry in front of her.

'I love you, I am sorry,' she breaks into tears, 'You are the best brother in the world.'

There are people who come to you and wipe your tears when you are in pain. They never let a drop come to your eyes. It is not just painful for Adrika, but also for him to see her going through the same situation he was in a few years ago. He regrets that he could not prevent it. He looks sentimental but courageous enough to control his emotions.

'Maybe. But you are the best sister,' he pinches her nose and says, 'You just get well soon.'

She bursts out, 'I am sorry. I have made mistakes all over again. Lied to you, mom and my friends,' her regret is visible in her eyes and words.

'It's okay. It will be fine.' He pats softly on her head.

'Just when I had started believing in love, he ditched me and ran away without telling me. I changed myself for him. I thought of telling you about this but…' Adrika wipes her tears and presses her lips tight. She tries hard to stop her tears but she cannot. It would have been difficult for anyone in this situation.

'Don't cry…' he pats and runs his fingers through her hair. He wipes her tears and a few drops from his cheeks too.

'I tried to save it even when I was going through a bad time. Those marks Anushka saw on my hand and asked about, those were not love bites. He had hit me twice. He doubted me just because I had an unknown letter in my bag. He tore it into pieces and threw them on the floor…I was with him because I loved him truly. I tried my best to work on this relationship.'

Arjun remembers everything now.

She drags herself into more pain holding his hand tighter as if she is falling. Her actions seem more painful than her words.

♥

Arjun feels helpless and empty listening to her words.

'You are a strong girl. You have seen the worst phases in life. Just be strong. Time will heal everything.' He holds her hand tightly and tears from his eyes drop on her cheeks.

'I am good for nothing. I think I am not the right person to be loved. Whoever comes in my life leaves me…'

Adrika gets disheartened. She is losing all hopes of being happy in life. After all that she had lost in life, she had finally managed to come out of it and had started making good memories. Those memories itself are turning into nightmares now.

If at any moment there is a sense of doubt in a relationship, it is not going to work.

She could have stopped this from happening if she had ignored the first message she had received from Sumrit at the college fest, the first meeting on the beach, the first touch and the first shiver when he kissed all over her body. She could have stopped this from happening. Unfortunately, she had fallen in love.

'Adrika do not say that. Just have faith in yourself. Remember what you said when I was going through the same situation? Let the worst time go. Good things will come for sure.'

'I have wasted so much time, I'll regret that forever…' she says and hugs him.

She remembers how she had hunched on the floor to pick tiny pieces of the note that Sumrit had torn and thrown. In the dense silence of midnight, she was not feeling drowsy and kept each piece as if she was solving a jigsaw puzzle. She took some time, as lines were difficult to match, though the meaning she had understood long back. She had paused on a line—Do not cry. Things will change in your favour and you'll smile again.

Remembering that night inspires her.

'I am always with you. It's okay…and you have not wasted anything. Just because something didn't work out between you and him, doesn't mean it was a waste of time. Maybe it isn't the right time, maybe it's not supposed to happen yet.

'And it's never a waste of time getting to know someone because you're also getting to know yourself at the same time. It's never a waste of time investing your feelings in someone because you're also finding out what kind of a lover you're capable of being. It's never a waste of time falling in love with someone because you're also finding out what your own worth and value is. It may not feel like it, but you also benefit from your losses, and what you gain from it can help you. Be thankful for the memories, be thankful for the experiences, and be thankful for the lessons you have got. Everyone is heartbroken in this world, at least once. Feelings may fade and people may lose interest, but always remember that life goes on and you can only grow from having your heart broken.

'If your intentions are genuine, if your feelings are real, and if your heart is in the right place, then it is never a waste of time because you shouldn't regret something that once made you happy. So whatever happened, do not doubt on yourself.'

Adrika hugs Arjun tighter and shields him in her arms. He kisses her on her head and makes her feel stronger. Sometimes words have more power than actions. Right and good words give encouragement.

'Did you tell Mamma that I am here?' Adrika asks.

'No, I have not told anybody. She will get worried. Get well soon. Go home and meet her,' he suggests.

'Yeah,' she wipes her face.

'Have this…' Arjun gives her a water bottle.

'Thanks,' she sounds a little comforted.

'Take care. Well, I need to go home. I think Ved will stay here tonight,' Arjun says and gets up.

'Okay. Send him but tell him not to shout with no reason,' Adrika says.

Arjun leaves while calling Anushka.

Twenty-four

'WHY DON'T YOU switch the lights off? It makes me feel as if I am too ill. I am getting better now,' she tells the nurse who has just come a minute ago to inject a medicine. The nurse smiles. She has become a favourite of hers. Maybe it is because she injects her very carefully.

'Yes, you don't need this.' She switches it off and leaves the room.

Adrika slides up and leans against the wall. In the dim light that is coming in between the curtains, she takes her notebook and keeps it under her pillow. Probably, she will continue writing tomorrow morning. She has found a way to pass her time before she leaves the hospital. She will be discharged the coming weekend. However, she does not tell anyone what she writes all day and all night. Not even Arjun who is lying next to her bed in the twin sharing room. That is the irony of life. We never know what happens next.

Yesterday, Arjun fell from the stairs in the hospital while going back home. Dimpy Aunty said this wasn't usual. Therefore, she took him to the physician. Probably she suggested him to get the check-up done and then to include the expenses into Adrika's bill for company's reimbursement. No wonder, only she can give these suggestions. She has done this a couple of times in her family too.

Moreover, Arjun has been feeling weak and there's severe pain in his body for a few months now, but he hasn't taken this seriously. He is irresponsible about his health. Ved and Anushka are true witnesses of his casual behaviour. He has become one of those people who need a mother to be around all the time, to take care of them. No matter how much he has grown up, but his habits show that he is irresponsible and immature when it comes to him. That he has realized and accepted just about a night ago.

♥

Loneliness is the worst. While Arjun has been a great moral support for everyone, he has been ignoring his health, and over time it has become worse. However, he now knows that he has to take care of himself first to stand with everyone till the end.

He had started thinking negatively when he was alone. He had stopped talking to his friends. Ved had asked him several times if he had any problems with anything or anyone. However, every time Arjun ended the conversation with an argument. In the middle of the night, he would get up on his bed, staring into the darkness. Ved had noticed that many times. He told Dimpy Aunty about it but, considering his busy schedule, she thought this was his usual behaviour.

Next morning, the doctor has detected that he is suffering from severe anxiety disorder and vitamin deficiencies, which need to be treated soon. His carelessness and irresponsibility regarding his health have led to this situation. Arjun should take it seriously before it leads to depression. Without any further discussion, Dimpy Aunty decides to get him admitted, and Anushka reacts as a positive reagent.

'I was telling you to stay over last night but you always have to work, work, and work...this is what happens when one does so much work,' Adrika says in sarcasm.

'It is amazing that you are suffering from vitamin deficiencies. Seriously? How old are you? 26 or 27 maybe?' she adds.

'Well, now you should be happy that I am here next to you,' Arjun says lying down. He continues, 'Well, I do not trust this hospital anymore. I think whoever consults the doctors here, they all suggest to get admitted.'

'Even I think so.'

They laugh together after a long time. This is probably not a happening place, but a good time for both of them.

As said in the beginning—it is not always true that opposites attract, people who have same sense of humour do too. Two mischievous people easily understand each other.

Arjun is enjoying his time. No work. No worries. Just the horror of an intravenous needle. Arjun cannot stand injections. Suddenly, the room smells strongly of a sterile chemical sanitizer.

Adrika makes a squared face looking at Arjun and pulling the curtains aside a little.

'Did you again spray the body deodorant around?'

'No. It smelled weird so just once…'

'It is your body deodorant that smells weird,' she says and rubs her nose. 'Why do you spray this deodorant all the time?'

'It feels good. Well, do you know that two-thirds of the world actually prefers a deodorant spray?' he replies smartly as if he has to impress her with his irrelevant knowledge on this.

'Yes, they use it, but not in the hospital. Weird you,' she says and continues writing something in her notebook.

Dimpy Aunty and Anushka enter the room, taking out the lunch box from the bag, which is not allowed in the hospital. Well, nothing is impossible when Dimpy Aunty wants to make it possible. Ved is busy looking at the daily health reports, sitting on the sofa.

'Good! You both are in a private room,' says Dimpy aunty and comes closer to Adrika. 'How are you? Getting better?'

She checks Adrika's fever placing her hand on the forehead. She moves ahead to Arjun's bed and does the same. Sometimes, some random, meaningless gestures have so much meaning. It feels so peaceful and complete when someone lovingly places a hand on forehead. That is all we need—a sign of affection and care.

♥

Indian mothers are half doctors. Actually, they are everything. Dimpy Aunty is one of them. They are the judge of that high court where everyone is a victim.

'Doctors should discharge you both soon,' she announces.

'I didn't deserve this place, because of her, I have come here. How does it feel lying next to me?' Arjun looks at Adrika, teasing her.

'So good...like fault in our stars,' she says blinking at him.

Adrika is going through the worst time, but Dimpy Aunty senses a hope of happiness on her face when Arjun, Ved and Anushka are around.

Anushka sits on the sofa, reading some random report kept on the side table. She never had any arguments in all these years of friendship before yesterday. Maybe it was because of Arjun's careless nature, which led her anxiety to come out in the form of harsh words. He deserves that. She is straightforward and never forgets things. Never. However, she is an artist. She does every possible thing to see the curve of a smile on his lips. Sometimes, she collects the broken pieces, puts them in order, and fills those gaps with beautiful colours. She is a great artist.

'Look who is talking. You are getting older. Who gets vitamin deficiencies and anxiety at this age?' Adrika continues.

'You and your gadgets have made you lazy. You should definitely give a call to his mom,' Anushka says to Dimpy Aunty but is looking at Arjun.

Arjun looks at Adrika and then Anuska, making weird expressions.

'I think so,' Aunty replies.

'Don't tell anything to mom, she gets worried about small things,' emphasizing on each words, Arjun almost begs Dimpy Aunty.

'You are suffering from the things which my grandparents had at the age of sixty. I mean really, anxiety and vitamin deficiencies?' Adrika wonders.

She makes him realize how careless he is about his health. She continues, 'Arjun, it's high time, get married. Else, in the age of early morning romance, you will be taking homeopathy medicines and doing yoga.' She giggles. She looks blissful pulling Arjun's leg.

'That I have started. Yoga is good for health,' he says sarcastically. Dimpy Aunty goes to the other corner of the room to check the breakfast kept on the table. She would replace it with the homemade lunch box.

'I think I should talk to Dimpy Aunty about you and Anushka,' Adrika whispers grinning at him, 'Should I? You don't deserve better than her...'

He replies, 'I know...now shut your mouth and keep quiet.' They are not sure if Anushka has listened to their conversation.

Dimpy Aunty comes back and sits on the sofa after scrutinizing the breakfast table.

'Don't think too much about anything. Let life go on,' Dimpy Aunty says. Probably that is the spiritual message she has.

'You are not as bad as I always thought you to be,' Arjun blinks at her.

Adrika laughs.

Adrika pulls herself up to lean back and says, 'You got me here and you got admitted yourself.'

'Probably this is one of the rare moments. All of us under same roof, isn't it?' he laughs as if he has cracked a good joke.

'That was really bad,' Ved raises his voice in between the boring television conversation he is watching after putting all the papers in the file.

Doctor Vaishali appears in the room.

She has spoken with Arjun quite a lot in the last few days. Initially, telling him about Adrika's improvements, and now telling him about his own health issues.

Her fish shaped tiny earrings reminds him of his family doctor, Rashmi.

'Good morning Arjun, hope you are doing well now,' she writes something opening the placeholder and keeps it on the side table.

'I am fine. When will I be discharged?' he asks. 'I just consulted the doctor to know why I felt dizzy and now I am here.'

'That's what we diagnosed. There is nothing major. You just need to take care of yourself. Make a proper schedule,' she looks at Dimpy Aunty. Aunty nods in agreement.

'I have no interest in keeping you here. Someone needier needs this place,' she says.

'Thanks, Doctor.'

'Well, I had a crush on my family doctor. Her name is Rashmi, you look like her,' he says.

Dimpy Aunty and Ved look at him in surprise. Vitamin deficiencies might have hit his senses also.

'But I cannot keep you here,' the doctor turns back and smiles at him.

'Arjun, stop it,' Anushka interrupts.

'It is okay. Take care.' Doctor Vaishali takes a few gentle steps to attend to Adrika before she is discharged in the evening.

Twenty-five

A month later

VISIBLE WOUNDS MAY go easily but wounds which are invisible, take time to fade off. Sometimes, they stay forever. They hurt. Dimpy Aunty had told Adrika when she was in the hospital that absence makes the heart grow fonder. However, when that absence becomes permanent, it makes you stronger.

Those red roses are wrapped in red ribbons. Kept at the same place. Silent and stable, but dead. Adrika stares at those dry petals and wishes they could talk to her. Probably they would understand her pain better than the people who promised to be with her and left her alone stating lame reasons.

She remembers what Arjun had told her once—that a successful relationship is not really a spontaneous and impulsive experience. You have to put effort, work on it each day. A sustaining love takes time, effort and energy. You should not take it as a liability or an asset, but you have to be very alert to know what you have to do to make it work. To take a relationship where you wish to, MAKE NO MISTAKES IN IT.

Therefore, love is not just a feeling, it is a decision that we all take in life at some point of time. She has done everything to save this relationship but Sumrit can now understand neither her nor a relationship that they both can make beautiful together.

Sumrit ended up being a coward who couldn't take a stand for someone who loved him truly.

♥

It is difficult to smile when it does not come from your heart. Her tears had all dried up. She felt alone even in the most crowded places.

Adrika told her mother about the situation she was going through before she could know from someone else. However, her very own friends and relatives started saying that she deserved the pain because she disrespected her family values. Falling in love is like a sin in the society if it does not work out. People start making allegations the moment you fail in your life. Very few people become your support and help you to stand again.

'I hate you guys,' she used to say when her friends troubled her or teased her when she was with them. She used to put earphones with no music on to just avoid others so that they didn't disturb her. Now she is searching for at least one person to share her pain and feelings with, and she is left helpless. Time has changed, and with it people and her life have also changed. Completely.

Nobody dies for anyone. She is alive. She can breathe in the open sky. She can include anything in her appetizer. She can walk wherever she wants. However, when she breathes, she feels the suffocation in the air. When she goes out, she wants to come home. She is afraid of going out. Something gnaws her insides.

She takes more than usual time to chew a bite when she eats. Nothing tastes good to her. Just to take precaution, she has to eat before taking the medicines that will heal her illness.

She has stopped replying to messages from her friends because everyone asks about her life and relationship. That makes her weaker. She screams later in her bed.

Nights are the biggest devils in her life. She can spend the days in uproar and tumult, but nights drag her back to her memories, which have become nightmarish now. That is the reason she is not able to recover. To avoid this mental pain, she wakes up in the middle of the night. She just sits on the bed doing nothing for hours and hours.

She has become overcaring about things after a failed relationship. She has become over possessive not just about herself, but everything that belongs to her—materialistic and non-materialistic.

Losing herself in deep thought, Adrika takes her old notebook from the side table on which she was writing last night. She turns a few pages and reads what she had written. She has started spending time reading and writing. Dimpy Aunty and Arjun have given her a few good books, which may give her some space to think positively.

Her cell phone rings before she finishes the last line. She folds the page and closes the notebook, pushing it under the pillow.

She picks up the call.

♥

'You always appear at the wrong time,' Adrika says to Ved over the phone. She tries to sound happy to avoid questions about her life and health that Ved may ask. Somehow, she has been successful so far. She has changed a lot in a month—physically, mentally and emotionally. Sometimes, she does not like questions being asked about her, even by Arjun, Ved, or Anushka.

'That I cannot help. Well, how are you doing?' Ved asks her with a cheerful voice to make her comfortable with sharing anything she wants to.

This has become a fact of time that if her phone rings around 8:30 a.m., it has to be Ved. The last couple of months have made him caring and more responsible towards her. He calls every morning.

'I am fine. Where is Arjun?' asks Adrika.

This is one the few generic questions she asks every day and gets the same answers.

Ved replies, 'Mr Arjun has gone for jogging. The boy is taking care of his health nowadays. It seems he has taken Anushka's words seriously to take care of his health.'

Adrika smiles.

Dimpy Aunty announces from the kitchen, 'Adrika, breakfast is ready.'

Adrika is staying at Anushka's home since the day she was discharged from hospital. Dimpy Aunty took her home insisting that she was capable of taking care of the three girls at home—Anushka, her sister Angira and Adrika. Initially, she did not want to go but thinking over it and discussing with Arjun, she agreed that she also needed someone to be around her.

'Go! Dimpy Aunty is calling you,' Ved teases her.

'Aunty, I'll just come,' Adrika retorts, releasing herself from the bed. She adds, 'So you both are coming today?'

'Yes, Arjun and I will come in the evening. I will message you once we leave,' says Ved.

'Okay. Now I'll go. See you in the evening.' Adrika hangs up and walks into the hall where Anushka and Dimpy Aunty are waiting for her to join them at the breakfast table.

She drags the chair with a rough noise and sits.

'Who was on the call? Arjun?' Dimpy Aunty asks causally.

Her sight is always there on all three girls.

'Ved,' she answers.

'Okay, so they both are coming in the evening?' she asks passing her the plate of bread.

'Yes!' she says, chewing a bite and mixing sugar in her tea.

'Good! Today evening, I have got someone to help me in the kitchen,' she says impishly. Expressions on her face turn into a smile.

'Madly, he enjoys your jokes,' Anushka joins the discussion.

'I doubt,' hums Aunty.

Aunty laughs. Anushka follows her and Adrika grins.

Dimpy Aunty wants to discuss something important, which is why she has invited Ved and Arjun in the evening.

♥

They all gather at the dining table, and relish each bite of the delicious dinner that Arjun helped Dimpy Aunty to prepare. Along with dinner, Dimpy Aunty brings her humour to the table. Adrika seems happier when she is around.

Ved blinks at Arjun. Ved has always told him that he will be a good son-in-law if Arjun makes her his mother-in-law. Arjun told Ved to shut up by saying, 'If you rearrange the word mother-in-law, you will get a new word called—Woman Hitler.' That fits her.

'Speak of the devil and the devil is here,' Ved says, teasing Anushka.

She appears in the hall. Wearing a t-shirt and a salwar, and her hair in a braid with a ribbon, Anushka looks like a typical Punjabi girl. Her natural jet-black hair curl on her forehead. She looks rather cute with a reluctant smile. Her lips are pink just after a bath, always ready to curve into a smile. She has the perfect arched eyebrows with beautiful eyes and red cheeks; her soft and flawless skin possesses a natural glow, almost radiating a positive energy. That is what they all love about her. Arjun smiles and gives her a place to sit next to him. They all make a group of five as they used to in college days. Dimpy Aunty is new to this circle. She has grown quite close to them in the last few weeks. Probably not famous, even not known to anyone else apart from these five people, but they share a lot of happiness.

'So, when are you joining office?' Ved asks Adrika while Arjun, Dimpy Aunty and Anushka are busy in their own discussion.

'Probably next week. My leaves are getting over,' Adrika says with a rough expression. She does not want to go back to Bengaluru.

'Why don't you take a transfer to Mumbai?' Arjun suggests.

Arjun is insistent on her coming back to Mumbai. It will be difficult for her to live alone in Bengaluru. At least for few months, she needs someone who can meet up with her frequently. At least, on weekends, they can spend a good time.

'I have already discussed with the management to give me a transfer to Mumbai stating family concerns. They said they have initiated the request and I have received a call from the HR as well. So just waiting for the final confirmation and joining date. Mom is also coming to see me,' says Adrika.

'That's good news,' Ved jumps into the conversation cheerfully.

'So when is Chachi ji coming?' asks Arjun.

'Once I settle down, then I'll call her.'

'Good, you can stay here,' Dimpy Aunty says.

'No, Aunty, thanks so much. You have already done a lot for me,' Adrika smiles at her. Dimpy Aunty has been really caring and supportive in these last few days. They both have enjoyed each other's company.

'I told you. I can handle my girls well,' she pats her on her shoulder. Dimpy Aunty drags her chair forward.

'You know she made chocolates last week? Those were delicious and mouthwatering,' she encourages her and appreciates her hobby.

Adrika always wanted to turn this hobby into a profession from the day she started working late at night at office, but suddenly a relationship changed everything and she forgot her likes, dislikes and hobbies.

We all forget ourselves when we are in love, and become like the one we love just to make that person happy.

'Why don't you start your own small venture of chocolates that you always wanted to?' Dimpy Aunty says something that nobody expected her to.

Adrika has discussed her hobby of making chocolates with Dimpy Aunty. Moreover, she always has a different grace and energy while telling anything related to chocolates. She has been an expert at her work which has always been her hobby too. Dimpy Aunty was being her encouragement.

Ved gives her a surprised reaction as if she is in a world of possibilities.

'But that does not sound easy,' Ved says.

Dimpy Aunty looks at him and says in sarcasm, 'You still have a scope to grow up.'

She also knows it is not that easy, but at least Adrika will spend her time doing something that is not so easy to do. She will not get any free time to think.

Arjun nods in agreement and says, 'I have told her so many times. It's time to go ahead and give it a try.'

'Yeah, maybe,' Adrika nods.

♥

While Dimpy Aunty clears the table, Anushka appears with a few cups of dessert.

Arjun is still thinking about what Dimpy Aunty has said. He thinks, at least, Adrika will have something to spend her time. It will distract her and help her come out of the situation she is in. However, doing anything on her own is a challenge and she'll have to compromise a lot. He does not know about the success rate of such a venture, but he agrees with Dimpy Aunty. Being practical, he also thinks about her full-time job where she is earning more than anyone does at her age.

'Yes, you should definitely think about it,' says Arjun.

Ved looks confused though he can imagine only good things. The utopia. Doing something on your own gives rise to a deep, profound happiness.

Very generously, Adrika avoids answering the irrelevant question she has been asked, 'You are expecting too much from me now.'

She smiles. As of now, Adrika is only concerned about her relocation to Mumbai, which is in progress for approval. She will call her mother also. In fact, Dimpy Aunty is happy with her presence but it has been more than a month of staying here.

'I can imagine you sitting in a glass wall cabin,' Ved says, keeping the index finger on his chin and posing with a thinking expression, like Steve Jobs.

'Why don't you write a book? You do write, right?' Anushka abruptly speaks out.

Anushka was reading her notebook a few days back when Adrika was not in the room. Later, she took her permission and read it completely.

'No, no. That is his work,' she redirects all the attention to Arjun and continues, 'He has one completed book in his hand. Why don't you talk about that?' Everyone looks at Arjun.

'There is nothing to talk about. Seven publishers have already rejected it, few more are yet to reply. I don't think any of them wants to publish it, else they would have discussed with me. I have lost hope because of the way I am getting rejections from publishers.'

'Yeah, I have searched about it on Google, and I think it should be purely commercial. So, they didn't even discuss it?' Anushka asks.

'No, they didn't. I don't want to get it published, that's not my wish, I just wanted to share the story that I had written for someone,' says Arjun, looking dejected. Arjun has written a book for Pakhi who left him alone without giving him a reason. He has been in the same situation that Adrika is going through now.

He adds, 'I talked to one printing press in Noida. They are ready to print a thousand copies.'

'What is the actual problem, why are they rejecting it? Don't they know your genuine reason to get it published?' Dimpy Aunty asks something that even Arjun does not know.

'I think they are not interested in true stories and it's not commercially fit for them, but it's okay. I have again worked on it and let's see.'

He becomes a little emotional; it is evident in his words. However, this world never cares about your emotions.

'One day you'll surely get what you wish for.'

'Let's leave. I have diverted the whole discussion,' says Arjun and looks at Adrika 'Well, you should definitely think about what I have told you. You have skills, you have knowledge, and you have experience. Time to utilize.'

Probably he wants her not to be distracted or influenced.

'Just a few months of experience. I am still learning things. I may think about it in the coming years but not right now...' Adrika says and pauses in between.

She does not have enough courage to make herself confident because she is still holding on to memories of the relationship, which has already drowned.

Rather than giving more explanation, she asks Arjun, 'So when are you going to publish your book?'

'Once he comes out of his deficiencies,' Ved pokes him. Arjun does not respond to it.

'Don't do that,' says Dimpy Aunty.

They all spent a good family time with Adrika and the next day when she leaves for Bengaluru to get her things back, she gets a message from Arjun on WhatsApp:

Success or failure is not in our hands, but years later we should not regret that we didn't tried. Believe me, this is the best time for you to do it if you ever want to do or pursue your hobby. I have faith in you and you are worth more than anything. See you soon!

Nothing could have been better than this encouragement. She needed it to get her self-confidence and worth back, which she has lost being in a relationship.

She replies:

Thanks so much, Arjun! Well, I want to know your story through a book. Get it published soon. And Dimpy Aunty is so sweet to help us selflessly.

Fingers go ahead to type, 'Why don't you make Dimpy Aunty your mother-in-law?' But she stops. She gets a reply from Arjun.

Yeah, she has been asking me about my book from the day she came to know it's completed and that a few publishers had rejected it. Though she has no idea at all about publishing, she keeps asking and suggesting me what to try next. My wish is just to spread my book for whom I had written it. I am not looking for any profits, or maybe I'll never write after that.

Well, need to go. See you soon. Take care.

You will. You too, take care.

Twenty-six

IT HAS BEEN a week since Adrika shifted to Mumbai. She has to join office as a Production Manager. She is done with the first level of certification, which has introduced her to the genetics of cocoa and helped her identify the various flavour notes and aromas. She thought it was not that important and she just completed the course because she got reimbursed for it. But now she understands the cocoa fruit further, its various origins, the chocolate-making process in detail, aspects of flavour profiling and the impact of defects in cocoa on the flavour profile of fine chocolates.

Just to avoid loneliness, she starts browsing random stuff on Google. She closes the browser ending up with a search—'Types of chocolates.'

Something strikes her and she informs the reporting manager over an email that she will be joining the following week, as she is unwell. She sends her a doctor's prescription, which states that Adrika needs a few weeks of bed rest.

She does not know what she is going to do with her life, but she does not want to regret even if it goes wrong. She never stopped thinking of starting something on her own after the fight with Sumrit when he told her that she could not do anything with her life. Those words remain with her. Then she remembers what Dimpy Aunty has told her, 'You can do it.' It is good to trust your own people more than trusting a stranger completely. Sumrit was a stranger from a nightmare for her now.

♥

The sound of her stomach rumbling catches her attention. She takes a plate of noodles from the kitchen that she cooked in the evening. It is 12.30 a.m. Adrika is staring at the small wall clock in the midnight silence. Night seems to be the time when she reflects inwardly, and her mind goes into a deep silence with numerous questions and thoughts.

She has always been obsessed with a green-facing view. Today, she has a green-facing view in her own place but that does not really make her happy. It is the irony of life. When you need something, you do not get it easily and when you do get it finally, it is too late.

Standing at the French window, she looks outside into the night, black as coal. The canopy of the trees makes it even darker. She remains numb staring into somewhere with nothing visible. Her memories pull her back into those moments where she does not want to venture. However, the more we run from reality, the more it drags us there.

'You cannot do anything in your life.' These words hurt her every time she remembers Sumrit. Maybe she has less good memories to recall. Words have the most long-lasting effect on us. They stay with us in our memory forever, until we stop breathing.

She diverts herself and closes the window. She again goes back to her work with which she can distract herself, rather than to her thoughts.

♥

Adrika has made chocolates many times alone and with many of her friends. However, this is the first time she is not excited but doubtful and a little nervous as she is making these for people who do not even know her.

She spent the entire day making samples of chocolates. She has audited and seen things at the production unit. Moreover, after a number of times, she has found the right amount of everything that she believes work as the best combination.

Being impatient, she finishes her plate of noodles in a minute and takes her pills, as it is already late. She has checked the fridge several times in the last twenty minutes.

It is human nature that when we get something more out of expectations, we start imagining. Then, expectations hurt more. Adrika fancies starting a company with her mother's name, which will produce chocolates and distribute them all over the country. She will give some amount of the profit to charity. That is the first thought that comes to our mind when we do anything. Adrika is no different. Maybe these thoughts give her some positive energy. She wishes for her dreams, which have thrived in her sour and porous life. She hopes her utopia comes true one day. If it does not, what more does she have to lose?

♥

Sitting and reading something about suppliers and distributors on her phone, suddenly she swipes left on everything and calls Mohan.

Mohan is one of her 1 p.m. colleagues with whom she goes for lunch at office. He reports to Adrika. However, Adrika is doubtful of taking his help. When he seems like the last and the only option to offer help, she calls him.

'Hi Mohan.'

'Hi Adrika, how can I help you?' he replies in the most sophisticated tone as if he has worked in a five-star hotel for years. Well, marketing people do have that accent and tone of being over polite, though it is irritating sometimes. It is just like the person sitting at a call centre.

'I need some help from you...' says Adrika in a requesting tenor.

'Yes, please tell,' he responds instantly before Adrika adds more. Nothing changes in his tone. Sophisticated and sensitive.

'I need the list of our distributors and retailers. It is a little urgent. Can you share it with me?' she speaks with a hesitant voice.

'I have to check if I have access to that panel. I cannot access it from home. We can check tomorrow morning.'

'I am not well, so not coming to office tomorrow,' says Adrika coughing.

'Okay, I will check and let you know. You need it urgently? What happened?' he asks something that Adrika does not want to reveal.

'Nothing urgent right now. You can tell me tomorrow,' adds Adrika, pretending that it is not urgent even though she needs it desperately.

'Sure. I can send a few right away…the ones which are handy.'

'Thanks!'

The phone call disconnects. She dozes off thinking that she is not going to leave her job because she wants to keep herself busy and that she will manage this in her spare time.

♥

Yesterday, she wanted to call Dimpy Aunty and Arjun to tell them that she has started something on her own but she skipped the idea of telling them then. She wants to tell them with a piece of cake and good news if it works out.

She has all the positive energy, but a pinch of insecurity as well. We all have that before doing anything big in life. She has to come out of it.

It's quite a different morning for Adrika after a couple of months. She has some hopes to make her life better, both mentally and emotionally, and most importantly, to make herself realize what she is worth.

With positivity, nervousness, various types of thoughts, curiosity, fear of not being presentable, and such similar ideas, Adrika reaches one of the chain bookstores in a shopping mall, which stocks branded chocolates. If she is able to crack it, she can reach out to thousands of customers who will buy her chocolates.

She steps in as if she is hiding herself, carrying a bag of chocolate boxes that she has submitted at the entry. Inspecting around, she reaches out to the counter.

'Hi, who is the manager here?' she asks, pretending to be an important customer looking for the store manager.

'Yes Ma'am, please tell me how can I help you?' the man at the counter asks politely.

'I want to meet him,' she emphasizes.

'Ma'am he is not here right now…' he looks at her, being quite courteous.

'Actually I am the owner of a small company which manufactures chocolates. I want to talk to the store manager to check if I can keep my chocolates for sale at the store. Once these are sold, I can collect the payment,' she tries to make him understand and turns about to take her bag saying, 'Can you keep these…'

The man at the counter responds in an apology and a generous look, 'Ma'am, you can talk to the head of products in this regard.'

'When can I meet him?' she asks.

'You can drop him an email, I can give you his card,' giving her a visiting card, he does not take further interest and walks to the other section where books are on display.

Adrika has prepared the chocolates with all honesty and passion. This is the first time and the first attempt at such a venture, and she has gloomy feelings. But she does not surrender at the first attempt.

She encourages herself and crosses off the name of one store from her list. She comes out of the mall and takes a rickshaw to the next store in the list she got from Mohan.

She has visited eleven by the end of the day. Though she only has disappointment in her hands. Tomorrow again she is going to cover the other area of the city with a different proposal that she has in her mind.

Twenty-seven

IT HAS BEEN more than a week since Adrika continuously got rejected by people. To be precise, seventy-three so far and there has been no response for things she has worked towards. Not even a single person has entertained her. The list only has cross marks.

Sometimes things look easy until you do them. The dreams she has started building up seem scattered. She is a determined girl but the things that are happening to her are terrible. She just needs one person who will believe in her idea, apart from those who have encouraged her so far.

Even yesterday, she went to stores to talk about her idea to sell chocolates at a lower rate than others but nobody seemed interested even after telling them that she is associated with one of the brands.

It is 9.30 p.m. when Adrika reaches home. She sits on an old sofa, which is hardly sufficient for two. In a deep silence, she hunches over with a sense of loss so powerful that her muscles do not respond to commands. She gazes into the distance, fixed on some imaginary future of a life without the love of her life. A choking throat and a shortness of breath forecast the explosion of emotions. The vision she has, begins to swim in front of her eyes as tears well from deep inside and course down her cheeks. She reflects on her mortal life, knowing that it will all be gone soon. Her eyes bleed with pain. She loses hope that anything good will ever happen to her.

Cursing herself for everything, she cries, squeezing a bunch of chocolates that she has been carrying the whole day in hope.

With a glass of water and a few pills, she gulps down the pain and hopes for a better tomorrow. She sleeps off on the sofa, coving herself with a sheet.

♥

It is still early in the morning when Dimpy Aunty hears some knocks on the door. It is likely that it is someone new at the doorstep. The knocks are her CCTV camera to differentiate between known people and strangers. She gets out of the kitchen and reaches the door with fast steps. The peephole is not of any help to her.

She opens the door.

It is Adrika—standing and smelling fresh of a Burberry perfume. Definitely, she has made her morning good.

'Hi beta, how are you? Come inside,' she welcomes her as if she has been waiting for her.

Only a very few people get this kind of a welcome from her early in the morning. Because usually others just come to read the newspaper or to have a cup of tea with her husband. Sometimes, she is mean to them.

'I am good Aunty, how are you? Where is everyone?' she steps in, leaving her sandals outside to avoid dirtying the clean, wet floor. She takes a perfect four steps to reach the sofa and drags herself into the corner, near the dining table. It is cold, it is the end of spring. She can smell an aroma.

'I am good. Anushka has left for work. Angira is getting ready and her father usually leaves for work at this time. You had your breakfast?'

'Yes, I had.'

'Do not worry, I will not tell you to cook,' she makes her laugh. You need a positive environment to share your feelings. Taking a long breath, Adrika says, 'I wanted to share something with you,' and waits for Dimpy Aunty to react to her words.

This caught all her attention. 'What happened? Is everything alright?' she asks, sitting on the divan kept adjacent to the sofa.

Things were good when Adrika was staying at her home. Dimpy Aunty had all the solutions to her problems. If not solutions, then at least she was an encouragement. Her loneliness had made her more possessive and an introvert over time.

'I want to start something of my own...'

Dimpy Aunty becomes more curious because she thinks Adrika has listened to her idea.

'That is very nice. I was discussing the same thing with Ved also. There was no point doing the work which is a burden if he is not happy. Realizing years later and regretting that time will bring in more frustration in life.' Dimpy Aunty looks more enthusiastic than Adrika who knows the kind of struggle she is going through.

'I can't tell these things to Arjun because her mother will think I am distracting her son,' she laughs to make her comfortable so that she shares her thoughts with no reservations.

'Nothing is working out. I have been trying for the last two weeks but not even a single person has shown any interest or is even listening to me completely. Everyone thinks that I am not serious when I tell them about it. They are not even ready to keep samples. Don't know what's wrong with them,' says Adrika in a discouraged voice, fiddling with the sofa cushion.

Adrika tells her everything that she has done so far. Dimpy

Aunty seems to be her mentor and listens to her carefully. She must have some suggestions, believes Adrika.

♥

Dimpy Aunty says, 'You have to remember a few things, Adrika. It is your work, and you have to put all your efforts until you start getting something in return. Remember "some". Do not expect a lot. Moreover, do not run for big brands because you are of no help to them. You need help. So reach out to those people who think you are a profit for them. Start with small ones. Moreover, even if you hit a few offline stores successfully, target social media. That's all you have to keep repeating in a loop. It's the time to achieve milestones and display them. So that others get to know. You'll get visibility.'

She explains her things at a micro level. Adrika agrees.

'Does that mean whatever I have done so far is of no use?' she hums in disappointment.

'No. Never. It is a wrong perception. Whatever time you have spent is anyway going to help you. Maybe not today, but tomorrow for sure.'

Adrika nods.

She continues, 'Do you know there are hundreds and hundreds of people who embark on their start-ups every day? But their problem is that they are all inspired from others and follow the same way successful people have already followed. That does not work. You have to think differently and do things differently. Make your own way. Who wants to go on a same trip repeatedly? Everyone wants to explore new things. Similarly, you make them realize that you are more business to them than yourself.'

These words almost snatch all the hopes Adrika has at this moment. Adrika is intellectual, courageous and an intelligent girl, but at the same time, she is not great at convincing people and catching their attention. She takes time to understand and analyse what Dimpy Aunty has just said.

'Listen! It is not that easy, but also not that difficult.' Dimpy Aunty has strong convincing skills. She knows the art of persuasion. Sometimes she says things that easily hypnotize people.

'You were the only one who was selected as a chocolate taster in a big firm among 476 students. There must be something different in you. Isn't it? Maybe there was some reason. Don't you think so? Do you know the son of Sharma Uncle? He completed his engineering from IIT and was recruited as a software engineer in the States, but he did not join. He started his own firm. Therefore, you just concentrate on what I am saying. This is the age to struggle and challenge things. I know you can do it.'

Dimpy Aunty has almost convinced her, though she has omitted the fact that the firm Sharma uncle's son started does not exist anymore. He works in the States now, as a software engineer.

'So, tell me one thing. Have you ever bought chocolates from a big store in a mall or somewhere?' she asks Adrika a simple question.

'A few times,' she says.

'But most of the time you buy it from local shop, don't you?' she asks her again until she gets her answer.

'Yeah...' she says, getting a grip on her thoughts.

'So go to that store and start once again with more energy. I am sure you will do it.' Aunty pats her on her shoulder and gets up to get breakfast and tea for both of them.

She suddenly turns back and asks, 'Have you told Arjun about this?'

'Nothing is happening, what to tell? I was calling Ved but he was busy I guess.'

'Okay. Do not call him. I will call him next week,' she grins and walks to the kitchen.

Twenty-eight

IT REMINDS HER all over again what Dimpy Aunty told her two weeks ago. She has followed her advice without any questions or doubts. She has visited thirty-six more stores in the last three days remembering what Dimpy Aunty said—you have to put all your efforts until you start getting something in return. Anyway, it is a defeat of life to lose the battle of love. The end is the worst part of a relationship, and you die a little every day. She has been living in that netherworld for a few months now, and she does not have anything more to lose. That is the moment which has made her realize that she is worthy enough to start a new life.

Adrika smiles, holding a five hundred rupee note in her hand as her first payment. She has received it from a small grocery store near her office. She gets emotional. A few tears of happiness roll down her cheek.

Though she has experienced that wonderful feeling of getting her first salary in her job, now it is even more special, it is something of her own. She is moving towards making a profession out of something that was only a hobby just a few months ago.

It is like getting your creations back in terms of monetary appreciation and it gives her a blend of materialistic and non- materialistic happiness. Both are important in life these days.

Her father always used to tell her that happiness is that state of consciousness which proceeds from achieving something through one's values and hard work. She is at that place where her work itself gives her happiness. There is immense pleasure and a different feeling doing anything related to it, she has started believing in it.

Adrika still has many things that she eagerly wants to discuss with Dimpy Aunty.

Now Dimpy Aunty has become the role model for her. If any day, Dimpy Aunty makes her résumé, Adrika's achievement should be on the top, probably in bold letters.

She takes her cell phone out of her pocket and taps the icon to call Dimpy Aunty who is now in her list of favourite people. Earlier, Sumrit used to be in her recent call list. She stops. She messages Arjun and Ved and asks them to see her at Aunty's place in the evening. Next, she calls Anushka to tell her that she will have dinner at their home.

Anyway, they all wanted to congratulate Arjun for the book that he has written. It is to be released in a fortnight.

♥

Arjun's face slacks when he enters and sees heaps of books in the corner of the hall. It has completely covered one side of the hall towards the French window.

'What are these books about?' Arjun asks Dimpy Aunty in shock, recognizing his name on the spines of the books.

He goes and grabs a book. His own creation is in his hands now. It is no less than the feeling of a mother who has just given birth to a baby. Arjun opens the book and closes it. He turns the pages and smells them intensely, as if it is his favourite fragrance which he wants to smell for a very long time. He inhales and there is contentment on his face.

Adrika, Ved, Anushka and Dimpy Aunty are sitting and watching him.

Arjun takes a few more books in his hands and walks up to stand in front of Dimpy Aunty in exhilaration.

He repeats, 'How did you get these books? No publisher took it for publishing. How did you get these?' Arjun experiences mixed feelings. He does not know if he should be happy or worried. He always wanted to publish his book with one of the biggest publishing houses. He wanted his hard work to be the base of his success. He believed that he would definitely get it if he deserved it. Else he would have printed the copies months ago. He had just edited his manuscript a week ago and started sending out proposals once again.

Aunty looks serious as if she has some plan in her mind or is making one.

'If you do not shout then I can share something important with you,' she says. There is a pin-drop silence in the hall.

'What?' Arjun doubts that she has done something extraordinary, which is not even relevant to him. Arjun recollects the casual discussion he had with Dimpy Aunty about his book. He takes the books again from the stack. Something strikes like a cold gust through his legs.

'Did you print the books?'

♥

Arjun looks at her expecting the answer right away. If his suspicions are true, then Dimpy Aunty has done a big mistake. He will never forgive her. Suggestions, opinions, perception are good to discuss over a dining table, but without his permission, how can she do that?

Dimpy Aunty nods with a serious expression. Arjun has not seen her like this before.

'You did?' he asks.

'You were discussing the idea about printing the books on your own and distributing it to the local bookstores,' Dimpy Aunty tries to convince him that she has not done anything wrong or illegal.

'What? So you have printed the books?' Arjun's expressions give away everything.

'Ya.' Dimpy Aunty says confidently.

Arjun does not know how to react.

She talked about the logic behind self-publishing a week ago but he did not agree with her.

'Yes, I was discussing the idea because I didn't know much about getting my book published. But it was my resolve to get it published by one of the best publishers. And you know that I have sent my proposal to some of them and one of them has even expressed interest. What if they accept it? I have come to know that one of the conditions says that, "No part of this publication may be reproduced, transmitted, or stored in a retrieval system, in any form or by any means without the prior permission of the publisher",' he says in a single breath.

Arjun speaks as if he has mugged up each word of the contractual term. Probably, he knows all of them now, after so many rejections.

He has the same passion for writing, as Adrika has for chocolates.

'But that term is only valid after the book is published, isn't it?' Dimpy Aunty questions back.

♥

Well, right now, the situation does not demand the discussing of passions. Arjun is on the verge of losing his mind. This is extreme. Half knowledge is so dangerous that it may lead Arjun into legal battles. She has put a gun on his shoulder and fired.

'So we will take the permission and I will tell them my plan,' Aunty says calmly and tries hard to justify her deed.

'Your plan? What is that? Do you know that it is to go against the law and it is illegal to print the book and sell? Moreover, in other terms, we are doing piracy of my own books, are we not?' Arjun does not want to shout but his voice expresses his sentiments. He sighs, regretting that he told Aunty to keep Adrika involved in something that could distract her. However, he did not have any idea that he would also be stuck in something that he cannot handle.

There is no doubt she has helped him in every possible way, but it does not mean she can poke her nose into everything.

Dimpy Aunty does not respond to him. They both keep quiet. Adrika waits for someone to speak and break the silence.

Then Ved retorts, 'Can we not return the books to the printer?'

'No, we will not return...' Dimpy Aunty interrupts. A woman who has always bargained to get more coriander and chillies from the vegetable seller will not do that.

Arjun must have not expected a business plan from her. Probably, this is her daring nature that forced her husband to start the business once again from scratch when he was bankrupt. He must be lucky to have her in his life. However, Arjun cannot say the same right now. He is enraged and is thinking of a plausible course of action.

Arjun responds to Ved ignoring Dimpy Aunty, 'These are useless for them. Who takes the things back when you have paid? No one.'

'So you have paid for this?' Arjun asks out of curiosity with no interest of talking to her and with rough expressions.

'Yes, do not worry about that,'

Dimpy Aunty is making him realize that she is following a proverb—do good and forget it by saying that 'do not worry about that.'

She knows how to play with emotions. She can trap him. Now he understands why his mother always tells him to stay away from her.

'Arjun, I know I should have asked you before doing it but you would have never agreed to this.'

'At least you could have asked me once. I do not know what to do now. How many copies are these?

'Two thousand.'

'What?'

♥

Arjun shoves his phone in his pocket and gets up to leave the place. Adrika tries to stop him but she has seen the anger on his face. He has never ignored Dimpy Aunty like this before.

'Listen Arjun!' Dimpy Aunty gets up and announces, 'I have an idea.'

He turns back with just a few words, 'I did not expect this from you. I already have hundreds of problems. You have created one more for me.'

His words come out harsh.

'Arjun listen! Just listen to me once. You three are always my favourite. I will not do anything that will harm you,' says Dimpy Aunty standing in front of Arjun. Face-to-face discussion has always worked for them—from his breakup to his writing a book to this today.

'I intentionally got the copies...'

Before he says anything, she continues, 'See, you are going to be a new author and who knows you? A few hundred readers? Today it is not enough if you have a good story to tell, and you have, and I have read it. Moreover, it's not that I do not respect your emotions connected to it, but why limit it to only a few hundreds? Therefore, why don't you do the same thing we discussed that day? Why don't you distribute your books at those stores where they don't stock books, with Adrika? See! Reaching to the audience who is already used to reading will certainly not help because they will compare your work to the many they read in their libraries. However, reaching an audience who can read but cannot get books easily, will surely make a big change for you. They will share the word with their friends. You have written a true inspirational story. I am sure they will love it. Be an inspiration for them too. I am sure it will work, and you should give it a try. And I want you to remember this when you become a celebrity years after.'

'Yeah, you should give it a try,' Adrika says in the same way Arjun did through his message a few days ago.

He nods.

'And always remember, for the publisher, you will be as important as the other authors. They will put the same effort for all. You have to make your own space, your own readers, your own identity. Nobody knows you. Make your own identity. You have to work on that. So, even if you get a publisher and your book is published by one of the publishers you wish for, then also you do not need to stop when it comes to hard work. Be good to your readers. They will do good for you. Word of mouth has more power than anything else. Consider all this as an investment for your future.'

Arjun carefully listens to her idea, it makes sense to him.

Rough expressions leave his face with hundreds of questions. He will be investing his time, but what if there are no returns?

'And how about giving a box of free chocolates with your books?' Dimpy Aunty asks and then remains silent wondering whether others will appreciate her idea or not. She tries to make fun.

Adrika likes the idea instantly. Maybe she likes Aunty's logic and confidence. Most importantly, Adrika also needs someone to walk with. Who can be better than Arjun? At this moment, even mental support is enough for her.

'What do you think?' Dimpy Aunty asks Adrika.

Adrika takes a moment before she pokes her nose into it. She wants Arjun to react to this question first. They have known each other very well, but she does not want to be a hiccup in his work.

'And how we will do that?' Arjun responds.

'Anyway, death penalty is the same whether you commit one murder or two. Let's try your idea,' he adds.

'You get afraid of things so easily,' Dimpy Aunty tries to calm him down.

'Probably I care for it. I am possessive, not afraid. If someone is going to ask me, I am going to tell them that you are the culprit.'

'Definitely! I am always ready to go jail for you, my love!' she says, punching his cheeks slightly.

Twenty-nine

IT IS 4 o'clock the next evening. Holding a small notebook in her hand to maintain accounts, Adrika, along with Arjun, has been visiting stores and the nearest confectionaries since morning. Arjun wants to clear the copies as soon as possible because he is still worried about the whole situation.

Even after dropping Adrika home, he travels with a bag of 100-120 books on his shoulders in the Mumbai local train. He has distributed more than 120 books today across the bookstores that stock only second-hand books, on the condition that they pay him post sales. He remembers Dimpy Aunty's words—first think about the visibility before your ego gets hurt by going to one bookstore after another. His father always says that nobody gets anything without working hard. That somehow encourages him at this moment. Moreover, his efforts will surely give him exposure. However, he is not sure if he will be able to recover the money.

Nothing is easy. You have to walk for miles to get something. However, neither Adrika nor Arjun expected this to happen. Half of the marathon they have already run, half is still left.

♥

'Now you should regret why Dimpy Aunty did not share this idea before,' Adrika tells Arjun while coming back home in a local train on one of the evenings.

'But anyway, this is illegal. I do not know what will happen when I get a good publisher, who comes to know about this,' Arjun is still worried but looks satisfied with the reduced weight of his heavy bag.

'When will we come back again?' Adrika asks in curiosity. She enjoyed eating sandwiches and drinking a glass of cutting chai on the street with him today. This will be a memorable day for them.

'Give them some time. Once the stock is over, probably they will call us,' he replies.

'Well, I have a question. They have kept the books in a huge heap. How will people buy when they cannot even see them?' asks Adrika.

'Hmm...'

They deboard at the station with a question left in Arjun's mind.

♥

A week later, after they have cleared half of the stock, on a sunny afternoon, Arjun is busy keeping away books in big cartons, putting one on top of another while planning visits to the other stores in Mumbai and nearby areas. His phone rings. It is Adrika. He attends the call. 'Arjun! Those three bookstores have called and asked for more books.'

'Are you kidding me? It has been just three days,' Arjun replies counting days on his fingers, 'Yeah just three days ago we had given them the copies. Did they say anything about the payment?'

'Yes, they said, "Give more copies and take your payment for the previous books'," Adrika says in excitement. Adrika is happy for Arjun and she is enjoying the time she is spending with him, learning new things. She is also in contact with a few hotels in Mumbai and chain restaurants to keep samples of her chocolates. She is going to make toffees, which airlines keep in the flights. She has been confident enough to talk and she has sales reports in her hand that she received from stores. This will help her when she will meet bigger clients.

'Okay!' responds Arjun thinking of all the good or bad possibilities. What if someone has filed a complaint against him and the police officer is waiting to catch him red-handed?

'I am also wondering, are you that great?' she teases him and continues, 'Well! I have good news too. There are a few hotels and chain restaurants that have agreed to keep samples of the chocolates. They have just given their inputs to keep the packaging traditional, like Hajmola candy, Kissmi Bar and so on. That I can do.'

'You have made me happy. Today, I'll sell fifty more books,' Arjun laughs.

'Well, I will go to some other places today. Are you going today?' asks Adrika.

'Yes! I am taking my last sick leave from office and leaving in sometime.'

'After that?'

'After that, I'll manage after office hours,' says Arjun putting more books in the trolley bag.

♥

Arjun takes the fastest bath and gets ready with a trolley bag, bigger than the earlier one. His expectations are higher now.

Dimpy Aunty has given him fake receipts of online orders from online portals to show in case someone asks about these number of books.

Arjun reaches the same bookstores near Churchgate station where he visited three days ago. Then he plans to go to the other stores. He prefers to go to the ones who called Adrika to ask for more books.

'Hello Mr Tiwari, how are you?' they ask in a cheerful and decent voice.

'I am good. So how are the books doing?' he asks in a thoughtful voice, controlling his feelings.

'Very good sir! Do you have more books?' the bookseller asks him and gives him a small stool. Getting a stool to sit at the roadside bookseller was not a small achievement for Arjun.

'Usually, on how much discount do you get the copies?' Arjun asks him calculating something on his cell phone.

'Sir, 35 to 45 per cent. That varies from book to book.'

'Okay! I am giving you more discount on the books now—70 per cent,' Arjun says playing a card. Arjun calculates if the bookseller is getting a profit of ₹70 from one book or if he is getting the same profit by selling two books. He will definitely try to sell one book and get the same profit because it takes half the space and less effort to sell. He'll take more interest to sell his books. More quantity will bring in more readers, which will spread more awareness.

Arjun gives him the books. He looks happier and keeps a bunch of books on display where everyone can see it. This is what Arjun needs. That's not less than getting a big hoarding of him. That makes him feel so. His hard work is being paid off. Slowly, but surely.

'Keep these also but these are not complimentary with the books anymore, because then it will be a loss for me,' Arjun gives him a box of chocolates.

'No problem, Sir. No problem at all. It will take just a few days to sell these books.' The seller smiles and asks his co-worker to check the previous and current balance amount.

The seller gives him the payment for the sold books and makes the day memorable for Arjun. He leaves with a smile and his heart full of satisfaction. Arjun skips the idea of going to other bookstores because he has no more books in his bag. He in on cloud nine. Singing an old song, he walks to catch the Mumbai local right away to meet Dimpy Aunty.

A Month Later

Arjun and Adrika's schedules have been fixed. They have been away from all unproductive activities. They have stopped watching movies and going out with friends. Some of them have started hating them. Arjun and Adrika do not care. They have thought about it earlier and decided that they cannot make everyone happy. So they just follow the path where they feel good and happy.

Arjun has begun to multitask in order to save time—he prefers taking a shower while brushing. This saves time; though not much, yet that assures him that he is utilizing his time better than others. He knows he has to cut down the time he spends on unproductive activities and need to put more efforts in order to get more output.

He may not have directly thanked Dimpy Aunty, but he is happier for everything that's happening to him. He is reaching out to more people and inspiring them with his words. Making people believe things, which may bring happiness into their lives, can give immense pleasure to anyone. Now, things look easier and positive to him. With a small step of initiation and hard work that he is doing with Adrika. Arjun is happy that Adrika is so involved and busy in her work and is also loving it. She is slowly forgetting the old hurtful memories. She calls him in the middle of the night to discuss the relevant ideas and then discusses the same with Dimpy Aunty. If things go on fine, soon she may not need medication to take her out of the trauma.

His phone rings when he is about to deboard the train. He picks up the call, stepping out of the train.

A heavy voice thunders, 'I am Inspector Panday, speaking from Lucknow. Am I speaking to Mr Arjun?'

He freezes and can barely breathe. He disconnects the call.

♥

His phone rings again.

Arjun feels his pulse beating in his ears, blocking out all other sounds, except his breath that is raggedly moving in and out of his mouth at gasping intervals. His brain has shut down. He is clammy and there is the glisten of cold sweat. His eyes are wide as if someone is coming to deliver the fatal blow. If he does not pick the call, he cannot defend himself. Being brave and changing his voice to a more confident tone, he picks up the call and says, 'Yes, I am Arjun! Please tell me what happened?'

'Why are you not responding to my calls?'

'Actually, I am travelling, so could not hear you,' he says going to a silent place near the ticket vending machine.

'I have called you to enquire about your friend, who has lost his cell phone. We got your number in the call list.'

'Okay.'

Arjun takes a long breath. He sips some water.

He has just recovered from anxiety after a long medication. He does not want to go into that phase again. He decides to clear everything; he cannot not live in fear. He has been scared for the last few days, after reading some news of piracy in the newspaper.

He calls Adrika the next moment and talks to her. All his excitement vanishes.

♥

Arjun rings the bell thrice in a row.

Anushka unlocks the door after a few more rings at the door.

Door opens.

'Adrika has got a contract from Holiday Inn and Taj Lands Hotels,' are Anushka's first words.

'What? Where is Adrika?' Arjun leaves his trolley bag aside and goes inside to see Dimpy Aunty.

'She has just messaged me,' Anushka says following him to the room and showing him the contract note on WhatsApp that Adrika has shared a minute ago.

'Where are you coming from?' Dimpy Aunty asks him, pushing his bag a bit, 'Is it empty?'

'Went to distribute books at bookstores,' says Arjun, sitting down on the sofa in the hall. 'Can you pass the water bottle?'

Dimpy Aunty nods and passes the water bottle to him from the table.

'So did he take the books?' she asks and waits for him to gulp down the water and answer.

'You know Aunty, those booksellers asked for more copies.'

'Really? Okay, we will print more,' she laughs aloud.

He laughs, 'Do not do that.'

Arjun tells her in detail what just happened to him.

'It's okay! You are not a thief. It is your book. If anything happens, you can tell the truth to your publisher,' she continues, 'So, all the books are sold out?' she asks in confirmation.

'Yes!' he says happily.

'Has Adrika called you? When is she coming? I want to

meet her. She has done things with great speed. She is so hard-working. I thought I was only the one,' he says.

'She was very happy. You both are working hard,' Dimpy Aunty compliments him.

'You are a businessman cum author. You keep giving more discount. If they get copies cheaper than what they are used to, they will stop taking old books and take only yours. And do not just stop here, even if you get a publisher. Buy your own books from the publisher and keep giving to all those bookstores you have covered so far until you become more famous. They know you and the strength of your story.'

Arjun bends down in salutation, 'So far, so good.'

Dimpy Aunty should join some marketing firm. The ideas she comes up with in seconds are insane, but have all worked out so far for both of them. Things get broken. You repair them and then they get a new shape, new name, and perhaps a new identity. Dimpy Aunty has given them that new identity. She has shared a secret with Anushka that during the afternoons, she calls all the bookstores of Mumbai as a customer on alternate days enquiring about Arjun's book and asking them when the book will be available.

She has created that flow, which was essentially needed. She has faith and believes that Arjun will maintain his storytelling and Adrika will achieve more success with her hard work. Her intention is to boost Arjun and Adrika's confidence because she wants them to see the change she has seen in them. She knows this will not help them build a castle but definitely the foundation from which they can build their future. Few truths are good to hide if they do not hurt anyone.

♥

Arjun enters Anushka's room while Dimpy Aunty is busy over a phone call in the kitchen.

'Hey come,' says Anushka. Arjun keeps looking at her.

'What happened?' she questions.

'Nothing.'

'So, you have done it finally, how does it feel Mr Arjun?' Anushka pats on the bed and gives him a place to sit.

Arjun does not take much time to say what he has come for.

He starts, 'I think that you have been placed into my life for a reason. Sometimes I wonder how I got so lucky to have you around. I have seen my worst and my best with you. People have come and gone out of my life, but for some reason, you never left. Your friendship is one of the greatest gifts I have ever received.'

Anushka grins looking at him and listening to him. She has wanted to hear this for a very long time.

'I'll not write a book about the positive effect you have had on my life or share it with anybody else. I would love to keep them as my fondest memories.'

'Okay,' Anushka blushes.

'Your energy and smile radiate whenever you see me. The care and compassion that you show for me is special. Many people tried helping me but I am so grateful to be affected and influenced by you, and you especially help me to get my self-confidence by your constant confidence in me.

'You know me to my core. You know what makes me smile and what ticks me off. You can tell in an instant when I am upset and then continue to do everything in your power to make me feel better. If I am going through something, you are the first person to text me to make sure I am okay. When my confidence lags, you reassure me of myself. You understand my odd sense of humour, my love for sarcasm, and laugh at my terrible jokes and side comments. I know, I am bad at jokes but you laugh at all of them.'

Arjun comes ahead and holds her hands. He says, 'I don't doubt Dimpy Aunty's skills but I always wonder how she is doing everything so perfectly and is helping me achieve my dreams. Why didn't you tell me that it was you, who was behind it knowingly and unknowingly?'

Anushka is not reacting to his words. She just closes her eyes and grips his hands tightly.

Arjun says, 'You believed in me when I didn't believe in myself. You loved me when it was hard to love me. You listened to me when I didn't have a voice and let me cry in your arms when I was broken. But most importantly, you never gave up on me. You have done things which nobody knows. With no expectations in return. With love and care. That is special. I know, I cannot thank you for this but I have wanted to say this for so long. I know that wherever life takes us, you will be a part of my life. Whenever I need you, I know you will always be there. And I will tag you in my heart forever.' He takes a step further and kisses her on her lips. This first kiss between them will be memorable.

There are a few knocks at the door before Anushka reacts. Dimpy Aunty calls Arjun.

Arjun gets up and walks to open the door.

'You are here?' Adrika pushes Arjun saying, 'Come, come, come…'

Ved enters and follows her to the hall where Dimpy Aunty is chopping vegetables and preparing dinner. Anushka also appears in the room.

'Aunty! See…' Adrika says showing her a piece of paper. Arjun closes the door behind him and walks to stand behind her to read the paper.

'What?' Dimpy Aunty says, taking the paper in her hand.

'I got the contract and hopefully I'll be getting a few more in the coming days, if things go well. My experience has worked well. I am going to apply for TIN (Taxpayer Identification Number) tomorrow, along with company registration.'

Adrika looks like the happiest person at this moment. Arjun keeps a hand on her shoulder and says, 'The company. You always dreamt of it, remember? You have finally done it.' His hand moves to her head. He is going to call his mom and Chachi ji to tell them about the first girl in their family who is making the whole generation proud. Expressions on his face say everything.

Adrika hugs Dimpy Aunty and Arjun together saying, 'Thanks for everything! Everything.'

'This is the effort that you both have put for each other,' says Dimpy Aunty. She winks at Arjun to tease him and make him realize that she is never wrong about the things she has done.

'You deserve it,' Arjun responds.

Ved breaks the seriousness, joining them.

Anushka comes from behind, and tries to join the group hug, saying to Dimpy Aunty, 'Do not forget your daughter.'

Arjun and Anushka look at each other, smiling. They are happy as they hold each other's hands.

'I think, I am eligible to be a part of your group which you lost in your college days. Do I call it VAADA?' Dimpy Aunty says, excited that she made up the name with the first letter of everyone's name. She is the new member in the gang of people who have failed in love, but have found what they love to do.

'VAADA—the promise, promise to be with each other forever.'

'VAADA.'

'VAADA.'

'VAADA.'

They repeat.

Epilogue

ARJUN HAS SOLD more than 5,000 copies in a few weeks after signing a contract with one of the biggest publishing houses. He still visits all the bookstores and gives them his books after buying them from the publisher. He believes that they have made him the writer he is, and they would continue to help him grow. Five thousand is not a life-changing number, but now everyone knows his name and encourages his efforts.

He has been listed on the Top 10 Most Influential Indian Authors list and is known as India's most popular storyteller of true stories. A writer who became a bookseller to become the bestselling author. Behind every successful man, there is a woman. That is the universal fact and in his case, it is Dimpy Aunty and the one he never talks about. He wants to keep her his secret success.

Adrika is currently reading Arjun's book and the note that Arjun gave her a few months ago when she was going through a tough time. This note changed almost everything in her life. Everyone goes through a tough time. However, what we take out of that tough time changes everything in life. Who knows that better than Adrika? She lost her father, was embittered by love and learnt a lesson after losing many things in life. Visiting many cities across the country in the last one month, she has started a new life.

She has set up her own small venture of making chocolates in Assam and Maharashtra that only delivers chocolates to very small cities and major chain hotels like Taj, Holiday Inn, Hyatt, Radisson and Lemon Tree Hotels. She has no plans of expanding it right now. Dimpy Aunty has told her that a brand becomes stronger when you narrow its focus. She just wants to focus on the quality and packaging for now. Adrika has a marketing team but Dimpy Aunty is the backbone. Ved has joined Adrika in partnership, and they both are managing things smoothly.

♥

Arjun pulls his luggage to the corner of the room and sets four alarms at 5:10, 5:13, 5:15, and 5:17. They are necessary for him to get up at 5:30 a.m. His cell phone rings. He disconnects.

'Arjun your phone is ringing,' says Adrika from the hall.

Tomorrow, 10 July, will be a big day for them. Arjun and Adrika have been invited for a TEDx talk in Chandigarh.

'Why were you not picking my call? I got worried. How are you?' Dimpy Aunty shoots questions in a row. However, everything seems irrelevant right now. Because firstly, he does not want to pick up her call, secondly, it does not matter to him whether she is worried or not because she is always worried for him for no reason, and thirdly, he is simply nervous. Not because of the speech he has to give tomorrow but he has acrophobia and it is raining a lot in Mumbai for the last few days. The possibility of a turbulent flight scares him.

'I am fine,' Arjun says in dry tone.

'Arjun, it's okay. It is going to be easy. Do not be nervous,' Dimpy Aunty says encouraging him.

'I am not nervous,' he says.

'Aunty! He is nervous because of turbulence,' Adrika giggles, shouting and entering the room where he is struggling to keep things in his bag.

'Thanks!' says Arjun.

'Thanks for?' Aunty asks.

'Whatever you have done for both of us. Because of you, we are here. I know thanking you is not enough for that,' Arjun rarely shows his emotions but his tone probably expresses his feelings.

'Then do not say thanks!' she says casually. She knows the hardships with which Arjun has lived—away from his family, suffering health issues and then managing everything alone. She just tries to support him with her bubbly nature.

'Where is she?' she asks.

'She is excited for tomorrow. She is staying here and then tomorrow morning, we will leave,' Arjun tells Aunty.

So, there are two people at Arjun's place when Dimpy Aunty calls him. They have been invited for the talk, for making a change and inspiring people.

They reach Chandigarh the next day.

♥

Adrika enters the stage greeting everyone and she is welcomed with a huge round of applause. She starts, 'Love is to be lived and understood, not controlled.

'It is learning, not domination. If it is controlled then it is not love, it is a compromise that the other person is making for you. Come out of that illusion. I have realized after losing many things in life. Well, it is good you do not get everything in your life, otherwise you will stop working for it. I am certain that I did not get what I always tried for, but I always got more than I deserved.

'A little less is always good, that way you fight for more. Make examples, and become an inspiration.

'An idea, which was initiated just for me to take my time away and distract me from my depression, was not so easy for me. That "idea" actually worked out because of a woman in my life—Dimpy Aunty. She is the inspiration behind my success. Adrika points out to the slide on the projector. Unfortunately, she is not here. Otherwise, she would have sat in the first row. Today is her day.'

She continues, 'I know it was wrong to be distracted by my past, but it becomes very difficult at the end of the day. You come back to the bed where your own memories start haunting you. I have cried over nights, cursed my life and asked God why He has given me this life. As we say, rather than trusting strangers completely, it is good to trust your own people a little more. I have trusted the people who are sitting right here. Thanks to you all! Well...this is the speech, which I prepared for today. Now coming to the point, what I really want to say...

'Love does not come with guarantee, it is like a game of bluff; if you find the right person, it works. If it does not, move on, just like in a game of chess—you have to move on from losing it all. Do not ruin your life for someone who does not care for you. Show your anger, show your pain, but do not just die. Do anything you feel like. Go wherever you want to. Do things that you have always wanted to do, no matter how impossible those seem. I promise you can make them possible. Because if I can, you can, and we all can.

'Love is not just a feeling; it is a decision. Decision, we all take at some point of time in life.

'"Do not forget your people whom you love the most and who love you the most. Do no hurt them." I remember, years ago, my friend said this in college. Today, I am speaking here; tomorrow someone else will speak about success and failures of life. However, what has been important for me in these years is that I had amazing friends with me whom I found in the initial days of my college life. I am blessed that I am still with them. They were my foundation. They motivated me to do what I loved to do.

'Unfortunately, in the race of life, we forget our own friends and family and then say life has changed, it is not as good as earlier. How will life be good when you are away from the people who helped transforming it?'

She looks at the camera, 'I do not know where my past is but I just want to say that—you are yours before you are someone else's. Thank you!' Adrika joins her hands and says namaste. She leaves the stage amidst the echoes of claps and whistles.

That hug between a brother and a sister, everyone remembers. Forever.

A note from your author

Everyone's life is like a book and we all live as characters of the book. At times, we go through tough situations and then at moments, everything inspires us to stand back. Just like a book, we all have a blank page in the end where we can give ourselves the perfect ending we wish for. Yes, life is like a thriller book and we all live like characters of the book.

Firstly, thanks to the whole team of Rupa Publications for discussing and answering my crazy questions. I am hoping to be more mature in the upcoming years. Bear with me.

Now, I would like to say thanks to my mother Kusum for blessing me with her good wishes. She has been so possessive about me since my birth that she named me Anuj (which means younger brother), to keep me away from girls. The moment a girl asks my name, it seems to be over. Thanks Mom, you win!

My father, Ashok, who has always been my inspiration to work hard, harder and the hardest. It would not have been possible for me to take ownership of the multiple roles I play, had it not been for him.

My love to Neerja for loving and understanding me.

Thanks to Dimpy Aunty and Anushka for transforming my life. Trust me, it is worth being with you. I mean it.

Thanks to Rahul Mohandas for discussing my professional and personal life, and counselling me whenever I needed him.

Love to the kids, Shivalika, Shivansh and Adya.

Special thanks to Sneha, Sandhya, Shraddha, Saroj and

Shivprakash for making me feel that I am never away from my family. You all are a family now.

Before I become any more sentimental, my heartfelt and genuine thanks to all with whom I am connected.

And, lastly, I intentionally write about my readers in the end so that I can end the book with my appreciation for them. You are always my strength. Thanks for making me something from nothing. It is your love and blessings that encourage me to write and bring true stories which inspire us. You all mean a lot to me. Stay connected. Keep smiling. See you someday, somewhere, sometime.

Facebook: www.facebook.com/anujtiwari.official
Email: anujtiwari.official@gmail.com
Twitter: @AnujOfficial